A Heat Wave
in the Hellers

Praise for the Darkover novels of Deborah J. Ross

"Fans of Darkover rejoice. Ross's literary strength [is] her sensitivity to human needs and talents."
— *Publisher's Weekly* on *The Fall of Neskaya*

"Deborah Ross…does a superlative job [and] perfectly captures the Darkover 'feel'."
— Sherwood Smith on *Thunderlord*

"This is the best Darkover novel in a long time.... It's a tale of culture clash, in classic Darkover style, a delightful return to a fascinating world, and a great read."
— *Locus* on *The Children of Kings*

"[*The Alton Gift*] is a must for fans of the series, and reads as if Deborah has been channeling Marion's spirit."
— *Center City Weekly Press*

"Ross is able to skillfully weave…a great story. Highly recommended."
— MyShelf.com on *The Alton Gift*

"A worthy addition to Bradley's original Darkover series."
— *Publishers Weekly* on *A Flame in Hali*

"Deborah J. Ross does [justice to Bradley's original work], admirably. I could not tell the difference between her style and that of Bradley. Her additions to Bradley's book and world are seamlessly cool."
— *SFSite* on *The Fall of Neskaya*

A HEAT WAVE
IN THE HELLERS

and Other Tales
of Darkover®

Deborah J. Ross

Published by Book View Café Publishing Cooperative
P.O. Box 1624
Cedar Crest, NM 87008-1624
www.bookviewcafe.com

ISBN: 978-1-61138-776-6

Cover design: Dave Smeds
Cover painting: Hannah M.G. Shapero
http://www.pyracantha.weebly.com
Proofreading: Sherwood Smith
Interior design: Marissa Doyle

To Vonda N. McIntyre

Table of Contents

Introduction

I n my early thirties, just after my first child was born, I hit
day job career burnout. A friend invited me to join a writers'
group. Although none of us knew what we were doing, I came
home from the first meeting so exhilarated that I drafted the
story I'd been playing in my head for the last year. No one told
me it was crazy to write a novel in six weeks with a new baby. It
wasn't very long, and it was utterly unpublishable, but it reminded me of how important writing had been to me since the time I
could hold a pencil.

I wrote a letter of appreciation to one of my favorite authors,
Marion Zimmer Bradley. To my surprise she wrote back, three
pages of single-spaced typewriting. At that time, the Friends of
Darkover held periodic writing contests and published its own
fanzine. I sent her a couple of stories (including "The White
Oudrakhi") and received encouraging feedback. When Marion
began editing the first *Sword and Sorceress*, she suggested I send
her a story for consideration. I threw myself into writing the
best story I could. She bought the resulting story ("Imperatrix,"
under my former name, Deborah Wheeler).

When I submitted a story for the second volume, Marion
telephoned me. "Now, Deborah," she said, "I'm going to take
your story, but I'm sending it back to you for revisions." With
that, I made the leap from all-or-nothing sale-or-rejection to

working with an editor. My manuscript returned to me covered in red ink, with comments like, "All thuds are dull" and "Overwritten." *Don't fall in love with your words*, she was saying. *Make them serve the story*.

The next Darkover anthology was *Free Amazons of Darkover*, and I ended up writing not one but two stories for it. The first was so serious as to be downright grim, a blood-drenched parade of suicidal honor and equally pointless last stands. (It's not included in this collection for obvious reasons.) The second one, "Midwife," popped into my mind and demanded to be written. The image of a Darkovan banshee (gigantic, flightless, carnivorous bird) chick imprinting on a human (in this case, a Free Amazon lost in the mountains) ran away with me, with hilarious results. I pounded out the story in two frenzied days on my mother's old electric typewriter. It was my first "attack story," one that practically wrote itself.

Marion didn't buy every story I wrote, but she read most of them. Juggling young children and part-time career, I was able to finish only a few short pieces a year, one for the annual Darkover anthology, one for *Sword and Sorceress*, and sometimes one that wandered around in search of a home. More editorial notes followed. I like to think I was improving, but Marion understood when outside critical feedback is helpful and when the act of writing itself, story after story, is the key to development. Perhaps the most valuable advice she gave me during these years was to "play it out," to not abbreviate or undercut pivotal events but to give them full dramatic scope and to explore the nuances of each moment.

In those early days, before authors had to be paranoid about copyright infringement, Marion encouraged other writers to "play in her sandbox," in her special world of Darkover. I learned to pay attention to what she had already created. Writing in the world of Darkover was very much like researching historical fiction. This wasn't always easy, as Marion used to say that she never let consistency interfere with a good story. In the end, telling stories set in her world was as much about respecting the spirit of that world as it was reproducing details.

Toward the end of her life, hampered by a series of strokes, Marion wrote in collaboration with several other writers. I was one she considered because she had watched me develop from a novice to an established professional. When she asked if I would like to work with her, I was just emerging from a particularly difficult time of my life. The offer was an extraordinarily precious gift.

We discussed the basic details by mail and then I drove up to see her for a face-to-face session. She'd been resting and was on oxygen, but she insisted on sitting up when I came in, and soon we were deep in discussion. I knew she had been very ill, but seeing her made her extremely frail condition vivid for me. One of my memories of that visit was watching her "come alive" as we discussed character and hatched plot points. Her eyes "glowed as if lit from within," to use one of her favorite descriptions, and energy suffused her whole being. It was as if she had opened a window into her imagination and invited me to peek inside. Her secretary told me that she talked for days afterwards about the visit and how excited she was about the project.

We never got a second visit. She died a month later.

Marion had been a rock, an anchor, an inspiration, a trusted friend, and a guide throughout my early literary career. I expected we would have more time to work together, despite how ill she was. I believed in the magic of that last visit. It was indeed magic. And, although I did not realize it at the time, it was also the passing of the torch.

I went on to finish that trilogy (*The Fall of Neskaya, Zandru's Forge, A Flame in Hali*) as well as subsequent posthumous

3

collaborations (*The Alton Gift, Hastur Lord, The Children of Kings, Thunderlord*). As I write this, I am working on *The* Laran *Gambit*. Another novel, *Arilinn*, is under contract.

I've also followed in Marion's footsteps as an editor. In 2014, the Marion Zimmer Bradley Literary Works Trust resumed publication of the Darkover anthologies, welcoming back fans and seasoned professional writers, many of whom had seen their literary debuts in Marion's anthologies. I co-edited *Stars of Darkover* with Elisabeth Waters and then took over the editorial mantle for subsequent volumes.

The Trust, which holds the copyright to Darkover, has graciously granted me permission to use my Darkover short stories in a single-author collection. Here are the tales that first took me to Darkover, from "Midwife" to "The Death of Brendon Ensolare," a twist on the story of the imaginary Lieutenant Kije, and which Marion cited as one of her favorites. A couple of early "bonus" stories, one never before published, follow those edited by Marion herself. Only one other story needs explanation, the very last, and you will find my comments directly before "A Heat Wave in the Hellers."

I hope you find the journey as marvelous and enriching as I have.

Deborah J. Ross

Midwife

The nest was empty except for a large dark egg. The second piece of good luck was that the entrance to the banshee's lair was partially blocked by snow and debris, which meant that the bird could not return without giving Gavriela ample warning. Unfortunately, it also meant that she was trapped in a small, smelly place until she could dig herself out.

Gavriela n'ha Alys sat back on her heels and considered her situation. She had not cried since her oath-taking, and she did not cry now. She should have waited at Nevarsin for her Renunciate escort, which had been delayed by bad weather. Gavi had thought only of her own driving restlessness and the quickening snowfalls. She refused to spend another winter snowed-in, no matter how precious the medical records she was copying. Her replacement, a smiling, self-sufficient sister from Temora, had already settled in, so there was nothing between Gavi and the trail to Thendara but a stupid rule about not traveling alone. When she had realized she was being tracked, she'd panicked and become lost in the heights.

Gavi ran sweating hands over her trail-stained trousers. Surely she could afford to rest a little, trusting that the avalanche had destroyed, or at very least delayed, her pursuers. She could not face them or outrun them, even if she managed to find her pack animal. Her fighting skills were barely adequate; her escort would have been a competent woman with a sharp blade and ready fists. But she was alone.

All the smiths in Zandru's forge can't mend that broken egg, Gavi told herself sternly. *And speaking of eggs...*

She went over to the brown oval, breathing through her mouth to avoid the stench. It lay a little distance from the pile of bones and offal. In the half-light she detected a regular pattern of bumps and splotches on its surface. The egg was as ugly and smelly as its parent.

Her eyes lit on a large bone that appeared free from shreds of putrid meat, the scapula of a chervine. She picked it up, reassured by its smooth, dry texture, and turned back to the plug of snow and gravel. The bone spared her mittens from being shredded when she would need them later. Still, digging was hard work, and as her body heat soared, Gavi shed her outer layers of clothing.

Once or twice she thought she heard a sound from behind her and turned, fearful that the banshee might have returned through another opening. She could not understand why the parent was absent—didn't banshees incubate their eggs? Even in the partial light, she could see that the lair had no other entrance.

She had cleared a space almost large enough to crawl through when the egg began rocking violently. A curved beak, glistening wet, emerged from a jagged slit.

Gavi's first impulse was to launch herself through the narrow aperture, regardless of damage to skin or clothing, but caution stayed her. What if the hatchling displayed the legendary speed and appetite of an adult banshee? It might seize her before she could draw her knife. Or, worse yet, what if it caught her midway through the opening?

Cr-rack! Fragments of shell splintered the rude floor. Behind the beak came a bony head, poking vaguely at the hole that was still too small for passage. The creature made a soft burbling noise.

Gavi gave a short, nervous laugh. "You stupid bird! Get your nose back inside so you can peck your way out."

As if in response to her words, the egg began gyrating violently, and the cries escalated to shivering moans. The movements became so agitated that Gavi feared it might topple itself and split its skull on the rocks. She remembered the birthings she had witnessed, mute and miserable, in her childhood village. Her Guild Mothers had wanted her to train as a midwife or animal-healer, but she would have none of it. She had retorted that she had seen enough innocents die and had changed enough breech-clouts to last a lifetime. She had fled to the Thendara Guild House to escape the cycle of pain and incompetence.

She had not added that she had *felt* each dying mind call to her.

Now the struggling banshee chick had got itself coiled around her guts in the same way. She could sense its desperation as if it were her own, could *feel* its fading strength as it battered its soft head against the unyielding shell.

"Idiot, not like that." Gavi put the chervine scapula down and stepped closer to the egg. She drew her short knife and thrust it into the shell, using the blade as a lever to widen the opening. The chick quieted as soon as she touched its prison. It was still wet with amniotic fluid but not as odorous as she had expected.

As soon as she had cleared an opening for the head, the

thrashing began again, forcing her to step back lest the thing knock her from her feet. Soon the rest of the neck emerged from the splitting shell, then a rounded body on two thick legs. Except for the scaled hide on its feet, the chick was covered with wet down and looked very much like a drenched fowl, albeit an enormous one. Even in the gloom, Gavi could see that it had no eyes. She stepped back, her heart pounding. Of course, it hunted by sound and detection of body warmth. Its head swung back and forth as if sniffing the air. Any moment now it would sense her and strike.

The banshee chick took an unsteady step and began a wavering croon. *Think, stupid!* Gavi shrilled at herself. *What do newborns need? Food, of course! And if you don't give it anything else, it'll eat* you!

Despite the loss of her baggage animal, Gavi still had her small pack. She lifted the flap and took out a packet of dried meat. Fighting to control her trembling, she held out a strip. The chick continued its piteous cries, rocking back and forth on taloned feet. She approached closer, dangling the food under its nose. Suddenly the bird crouched, belly low to the floor, and opened its mouth.

"Look, stupid," Gavi said as she dropped the jerky into the chick's gaping beak. "Here it is. Who would have thought you'd need hand-feeding, a big, ugly brute like you?" The parent banshee would be doing the feeding under normal circumstances.

The chick swallowed the meat strip in a single gulp and resumed its begging posture. Gavi shook her head and fed it another, and then another. She was no longer trembling, but now she grew concerned about her food supply. If it was satisfied with everything she had, it might not attack her, but what would she eat before she could reach help? And if her meager hoard was not enough, it might decide she would make a fine dessert.

The chick gobbled all the meat plus some dried fruit and porridge meal, then closed its beak with a resounding snap. Still keeping its visibly bulging belly to the ground, it sidled up to her. Gavi told herself that this could not be an attack stance, and forced herself to stand still. The chick's down was beginning to dry and to fluff out as it rubbed against her boots and thighs. She found herself tempted to touch the soft feathers. Repulsive as it might be to her human eyes, she supposed the gangling thing must be appealing to an adult of its own species.

Evanda and Avarra, it thinks I'm its mother!

"No! I may have helped get you out of the Zandru-cursed shell, but I won't be a nursemaid to you, or anything else!"

But it was clearly no use. She had fed it, and spoken to it, and now it brushed against her legs in a fumbling caress, anchored to her body warmth. Banshees had a reputation of being as stupid as they were deadly, and sheer instinct had imprinted her upon this one's brain as its sole source of food and love.

"I suppose that's one small grace," she said, moving toward the lair's opening. "If you think I'm your mother, you won't try to eat me. There's just a little more to clear away here. No, don't butt me with your head, you silly bird. You'll start a slide and bury us both! Get *back!*"

As the chick lunged past her, she grabbed it with both hands around its thin neck. The down looked fluffy, but was covered with a sticky film. As soon as she touched it, the bird ceased struggling and took up its loving croon.

"Shut up. Just don't get in my way, and we'll both be free. I can be on my way to Thendara, where any reasonable woman would want to be for the winter, and you can be somewhere else, as high and as far away from me as you can get. Understand?" The banshee chick rubbed its head against her hip and intensified its hum of devotion.

Gavi pulled herself through the hole, noticing with some exasperation that she had made it amply large for the chick. While it wriggled and flapped through the opening, she got to her feet and looked around. There was no sign of her chervine on the new snow, but neither could she see any trace of her followers. The red sun had dipped well toward the horizon.

She still had some time before dark, and should waste none of it. With nightfall would come deathly cold and hunting banshees, if she should still be above the tree-line. She pulled on the last of the clothes she had shed during her dig, then oriented herself as best she could by the position of the sun and slope of the mountainside, and began to climb down. The chick flopped after her, wailing in distress.

"Oh, stop it. I'm not your mother. It's no good pretending that I'm a heartless brute for abandoning you. You belong here, and I don't. Get busy hunting something else. Shoo!" She made fending motions with her hands, and the infant halted, swinging its head from side to side in puzzlement. In the full light of day, it was even uglier than she had realized.

"I don't have time for this; I've got to be going. No, don't start that racket again. I can't take you with me. Poor thing, I know the light makes you sleepy—so go find some place to curl up, and let me be about my business."

Finally, seeing the chick resume its belly-down posture of adoration, she screamed, "Get out of here, you disgusting thing!" with such feeling that the creature, whimpering mournfully to itself, retreated to the mouth of its lair.

She passed the tree-line before dark, cold and scratched from a tumble on loose rock. One ankle throbbed ominously, her elbow was bruised and swollen, and her mittens were torn, but on the whole she had come off lightly. She was able to force down a portion of her food and find a sheltered spot beneath the branches of an evergreen grove. She made a bed of the dry fallen needles and buried herself in them for warmth.

Gavi awoke chilled on one side. A rather large and soft lump had planted itself along the length of her legs. She wrinkled her nose as a distinctive odor reached her, and opened her eyes.

The banshee chick, now noticeably larger than the day before, butted its head against her, warbling contentment.

"You stupid bird, what are you doing here? No, you're not allowed to follow me. Oof! Idiot, get off my foot! You belong up there, above the tree-line, and you're supposed to be nocturnal." She got to her feet and surveyed the fawning monster.

"You seem to have done well enough without me. All that gore on your chest must be leftovers from dinner last night. Ugh! Your table manners could be improved. No, I won't let you near me until I've cleaned you up a bit. Hold still!"

The pine needles were absorbent and would make the thing smell better. She discarded the last handful of soiled leaves and pushed the chick away.

"Now go, do you hear me? I don't want you! Scat!"

The chick sidled a few steps away, the heat-sensing eye spots on its skull shining in the wan sunlight. The croon degenerated into a mournful sob.

Gavi could not suppress a smile. "You do make the most ridiculous noises, but that makes no difference. Off you go!"

She turned on her heel and proceeded down the slope.

She knew the bird was following her, keeping hidden in the shadowed shelter of the rocks. Banshees were torpid by day, and the direct sunlight must make any activity difficult. *If only the thing would give up and go back where it belonged!* she fumed, wondering if she had created a perverted, daytime, human-loving monstrosity.

Before long she found the trail of wild mountain chervines, and knew that it would lead to a source of water. Upon examining the prints, she detected the impression of shod hooves. If Evanda's own luck were with her, her pack animal had survived, and she stood a chance of recovering her food and gear. She quickened her pace along the trail.

She stumbled into the camp without warning. Just a turn off the main path, and suddenly she was practically in the lap of a strange man, hastily rising from a cook-fire. It was too late to rectify her error. She had been so preoccupied with escape from the banshee and finding her lost pack animal that she had forgotten the men who had shadowed her the day before. She knew she could not hold her own against multiple experienced attackers. Against one, maybe. Her small knife felt steady and solid in her hand.

The man before her, wiping his hands on his homespun breeches, was clearly no bandit, and he seemed to be alone. Gavi let the tip of her knife drop but did not relax her fighting stance. Her eyes lit upon her chervine, tied to a branch on the far side of the fire, partially unloaded. Her precious warm clothing and blankets lay scattered on the dirt.

"That's my animal and my pack."

The herdsman's face reddened in a twisted grin, showing badly decayed teeth. "Ho-oh-oh!" he exclaimed in a thick provincial accent. "Finder keeps all, that's the law of the hills. You be stranger, p'raps you not know the law. Who be your man?"

"I am a free woman, a Renunciate. I answer to no man."

"Naw! But yet, I have hear of such. Lordless wenches you be. A bedding and a beating will soon lesson you, ho-oh-oh! Unless you relish them in the reverse order." he guffawed, obviously much impressed by his own humor.

Gavi pressed her lips together in revulsion. And she had thought the banshee chick ugly! It was only a natural creature, bound by instinct. It meant her no personal harm and knew no better, whereas the man before her, sniggering as he approached, had at least the outward seeming of rationality, yet was incapable of decency or honor. She thrust out her knife so she could be sure he saw it.

"I warn you, I am prepared to defend myself!"

He halted, but his unpleasant expression did not change. "What, with that little pin-sticker?" He chuckled, looking down at his expanse of fat-cushioned gut. "Naw, wouldn't do more than scratch. Might be good for pickin' teeth afterward."

Gavi fought to keep from trembling, realizing the weakness of her position. One part of her mind kept arguing, *He's trying to bully you into defeat, so don't listen to him! A Free Amazon never gives up, haven't you learned anything? What would your Guild sisters say to that? You can still aim for a vital target. His fat won't protect his throat or eyes. You can use his own weight against him!* But her psychological defenses had been breached, and she knew he could see the despair in her eyes.

The same fury that had driven her from her father's house to

13

the gates of the Thendara Guild House boiled up in Gavi's heart. *No!* she stormed. *I will not be cowed like some dumb beast! I've little skill as a fighter, but if I cannot stop him any other way, it's my corpse he'll have to rut on. May Avarra have mercy on my soul!*

She took a step backwards, considering flight and discarding the idea. She was weakened from her night of exposure, and to be caught from behind would sacrifice any slim fighting advantage she might have. She tightened her grip on her small knife and took a breath. There was still a chance she could stun him enough to escape.

The herdsman made a quick movement, closing the distance between them by half. Gavi could not have outrun him, even panic-fueled. She prepared for the shock of his attack when suddenly the air shattered with a horrendous ululating cry. It stunned her, freezing her heart and almost causing her to drop her knife. Again came the shriek, so close she could not determine its direction.

The effect upon the man was equally astounding. Color evaporated from his face, leaving him ashen white, and he began to tremble violently. "Banshee," he whispered. "Ach, 'tis doom for sure, to hear a banshee under the bloody sun."

"'Tis *doom for sure* to lay a finger on me or mine!" Gavi cried. "Did you think I meant to defend myself with this knife alone? Get you gone before I summon the demon to swallow you up!"

For a moment, she feared that his native shrewdness would give him pause, but his wits had fled along with his ruddy complexion. He vanished down the trail, leaving the remains of his own camp behind. Gavi did not stop shaking until he was well out of sight.

The wailing came another time, softer and more defined in direction. She could see the chick above her now, moving down with unexpected grace. The chervine whickered, its eyes rolling in fright, and pulled at its tether. Gavi petted it soothingly.

"No, stop, you dumb bird! You'll scare the wits out of my baggage, and then I'll be right back where I started. All right, I'll come up to you. Just stay there!"

The chick seemed to have grown since the morning, its feathers smoother and less fluffy. Its hunting wail died into a croon of ecstasy as she approached it.

Relief swept away terror as Gavi bent to the banshee, her arms encircling it. It was long minutes before she could sob, "Oh, you ridiculous, disgusting bird, you saved me! I was dumb enough to travel without an escort, and you volunteered to be mine."

She sat back on her heels. "What am I to do with you now? I can't stay here, not even if I wanted to, not with winter coming on. No, stop butting me with your beak, it's sharp! Listen, idiot—oh, who's the idiot? Me for breaking a rule meant to protect me, or you for thinking I'm your mother?"

The banshee, still humming in delight, snaked its neck along the side of her thigh. She stroked it hesitantly, feeling the oiled smoothness of the feathers overlying its baby down.

"You truly can't come with me," she said in a soft voice. "You shouldn't even be awake now. It's unhealthy for you. And you've got to go back to the heights where you belong, just as I've got to return to Thendara." She had grown attached to the infant, ugly though it might be. She had helped birth it, fed it, cared for it, spoken to it as a companion...and now she must let it go. She must make it return to its natural environment. But how? Scolding had not deterred it, although she owed her life to that failure.

Gavi took the hideous head in her hands, carefully avoiding

the sensitive eyespots. She fumbled in her heart for the words that would make parting as much an act of love as following.

"You must go your own way, my friend, as I must go mine. Not because you are ugly in my sight, or because there is no bond between us. But rather because your life must be up there, you can flourish. You are a child of the gods, no less than I, and they have made us different. Return to your own place with my blessing. *Adelandeyo.* Go in peace."

The banshee chick huddled still and warm by her side, its croon thrumming like a heartbeat. Gavi could see no flicker of response or of comprehension. Why had she expected it would understand? Banshees were so stupid as to be practically brainless, she had always been told. It was the victim's own paralysis that enabled them to survive.

The chick dropped its beak with its wicked hook and razor serrations, caressing her thigh with the polished outer surface. Then it heaved itself to its feet and departed upward with surprising speed. Gavi watched until it was out of sight, then rubbed her hands and clothing with scented leaves before approaching the chervine again.

As she shook out and repacked her clothing and sleep roll, Gavriela thought, *It couldn't have understood me, but it did. If I can midwife a banshee, I can learn to love anything. Maybe I spoke to it in the same way it reached me from the shell. The Guild Mothers were right, I ought to be using my gifts, but not for watching babies die...for helping them live. But they'll never believe the birthing that taught me that lesson!*

The chervine butted her with its soft nose as she led it down the slopes toward Thendara and home.

The Death of
Brendon Ensolare

"Hey, Raimon! Welcome back, you old *cralmac!*"

"Same to you, Edric." Raimon Valdizar grinned, showing white teeth in a darkly handsome face, and clapped his friend on the shoulder. At sixteen, he was one of the younger third-year cadets who stood a little apart from the mature guardsmen, waiting for the formal ceremony that would begin the Comyn Council season. "Anyone seen Bredan yet?"

"Didn't he stay with your family over the break?" asked Felix Macrae, a slender youth with reddish tints in his strawberry hair.

"Yes, and damned near convinced my parents to hand-fast my oldest sister to him," Raimon laughed. "But she didn't care for his freckles." Lanna actually liked Bredan well enough, but was too spirited to do anything that would please her older brother without putting up a token resistance. She knew that nothing would suit Raimon so much as the *bredu* of his heart becoming his brother in truth.

"Who's cadet-master this term?" someone wanted to know.

"Not Di Asturien again. I heard one of the officers say he's temporary commander," Edric said.

"They ought to let the old man retire. He must be almost
ninety. Even the Comyn can't expect—"

"Bredan, quick! You're just in time. We're about to start!"
Raimon grabbed his arm and pulled him into line. Bredan
Escobar was wiry and good-looking, a golden shadow to
Raimon's darkness.

The old man walked into the hall with stately grace and the
entire assembly—officers, mature guardsmen, and cadets—
came to attention. The first-year cadets, brazen and unsure,
stood in a little knot where the light from the great fan-shaped
windows highlighted their multicolored civilian clothing.

Raimon heard their muttered comments and glared at them.
*They think he's a doddering old fool. They don't know how lucky they are
to have him now that Lord Alton's gone off-planet with his son. We could
have Dyan Ardais, or worse! Di Asturien may not be as young as some,
but at least he's honorable.*

Domenic Di Asturien finished his opening remarks and
began the formal process of the roll. He held himself as proudly
as any officer in the full strength of youth as each guardsman
came forward and repeated the ancient ritual of loyalty. It took a
long time to go through the list and toward the end the pauses
grew longer, and the old soldier's voice less sure.

The next order of business was for the cadets to stand forth
in order of seniority.

"Valentine-Felix, Cadet Macrae…"

"Here, sir!" Felix answered, with more enthusiasm than
necessary.

The old man looked up, his eyes reddened with strain of so
much reading in the difficult polychromatic light. For a moment
he seemed uncertain. Or was he, Raimon wondered, remembering some other cadet who had stood before him in this very

hall, long since grown from boyhood with sons of his own?

The roll went on until Di Asturien stumbled again, over a name that was no quite legible. "Bre-Brendon, Cadet Ensolare."

Bredan cleared his throat, "I think—" he began, clearly meaning to say, "I think there's been a mistake." But he could not bring himself to shatter the illusion of the old man's competence.

"Here," he finished lamely.

At the same moment, Edric MacAnndra burst out, "That's Bredan, Cadet Escobar, sir."

"Bredan, Cadet Escobar?"

"Here, sir," said Bredan, confused.

The old man glanced down at the parchment in his hands. "Then where's Cadet Ensolare? His name has been omitted from his list. See to the correction, cadet-master."

Gabriel Lanart-Hastur, standing at Di Asturien's elbow, nodded gravely.

After the ceremony, the third-year cadets returned to the barracks to unpack the belongings they had taken home over the break and prepare for dormitory inspection.

"Hey, Bredan, one of you is not enough for us, eh? You had to be signed up for the guards twice!" laughed Edric.

"You!" Bredan rounded on the taller boy. "You should have kept your fool mouth shut and everything would have straightened out! Now we're stuck with an imaginary thirteenth cadet— what are we going to do when Brendon, Cadet Ensolare, fails to show up for his assigned arms practice?"

"I—I was only trying to help!"

Raimon said equably, "There's no harm down, Dan. Di Asturien may have ordered the name of Ensolare to be added to the lists, but the other officers know he doesn't exist. They'll fix things up quietly and we'll never hear of him again."

The next morning the assignments for arms practice were posted. Raimon elbowed his way forward to peer at the list.

"Oh, my aching backside, I've got Padraik for sword, and right before dinner," he groaned. "I'll never get out in time for a decent meal. You banshees will have eaten it all by the time he's finished with me, assuming there's anything left of me to even want dinner." Then he noticed the expression on Bredan's face. "What's the matter, who've you got?"

"Rai. Look!" Bredan pointed halfway down the schedule, where Brendon, Cadet Ensolare, was scheduled for a lesson with a new instructor, Timas Wellsmith. "You said they'd catch the mistake. We'd seen the last of him—your very words."

Raimon grinned engagingly and shrugged.

"I feel responsible for this whole mix-up," Bredan said. "I should go in and straighten it out."

"Tell Di Asturien he's made a mistake? To his face?"

"He's right, you know," said Mikhail Castamir, a serious boy from the Kilghard Hills. "We can't let the commander be humiliated that way, even if you told him in private. And he would be, if he learned he'd made a mistake like that."

"I can't just let it go on," Bredan protested.

"Look." Raimon took him by the shoulders, his voice soothing and persuasive. "It was a simple mistake, not anyone's fault, let alone yours. Let's get out of here, before all there is left of breakfast is cold nut-porridge with no honey. Besides," he added, as they trooped down to the refectory, "I have an idea of how some good might come of the situation after all."

Later that afternoon, Raimon, clad in old clothing and carrying a battered sword, presented himself for arms practice. Timas Wellsmith, he had learned, was a former guardsman who had tried breeding chervines, but turned out to be allergic to their dander and was forced to return to the only occupation he knew.

"Cadet Ensolare?"

"Well, not exactly," Raimon said, flashing his most engaging grin. "He had an emergency of an, um, personal nature, and rather than inconvenience you by being late, he asked me to trade session times with him."

Timas looked dubious. Perhaps, Raimon thought, in his day such things weren't done—you showed up for your assigned workout even though you were blind, lame, and loaded with *kireseth*. As a point of fact, switching times was occasionally although unofficially allowed, but any change in instructors was definitely not, and Raimon knew it. He tried to look earnest as he said, "I know I won't disappoint you, sir. I've been looking forward to the opportunity of training with you ever since we heard you'd rejoined the guards."

Finally Timas nodded, his features softening a little. "All right, then, lad, let's see what today's cadet standards are like."

At dinner that night, Raimon took his usual place between Bredan and Felix, looking very much like the proverbial cat set to guard the dairy.

"I thought you had the last shift with Padraik," Bredan said.

21

"And I can't imagine he let you off early for the sake of your empty stomach. How did you manage this one—you didn't cut training, did you?" That would be a serious breach, even for a cadet with Raimon's reputation.

"Oh," Raimon replied airily as he dabbed his stew with a hunk of bread. "I swapped times with our old friend, Brendon Ensolare."

His sworn brother gazed at him wide-eyed, and for a moment Raimon was afraid that he'd outraged even Bredan's sense of propriety. But Bredan was doing his best to suppress a whoop of delight. "You didn't!"

"I did, Aldones's own truth. I have a feeling this is just the very beginning—for all of us—"

Bredan protested, laughing, "The last time you got one of these ideas, we ended up with a solid month of latrine duty."

"I remember that," growled Mikhail from the other side of the table. "I still don't understand how you managed to talk me into it, let alone Felix."

Raimon refused to be baited. "But it was worth it, wasn't it, to see the first year cadets' faces the next morning? Even you enjoyed sneaking into the Terran Zone to buy the voice recorder."

"Whoo!" chortled Bredan, relishing the memory of his *bredu's* most notable prank. "You set the thing to go off just past midnight. *Beware, this dormitory is haunted! Beware the ghost who stalks these halls!* Complete with rattling chains and a great rendition of a banshee. They looked like they'd actually *seen* a ghost!"

Felix, sitting on Raimon's other side, said shyly, "How do you think of such things, Rai?"

"I stay awake all night plotting them. Now, I've been thinking—"

"I have a feeling we're going to be very, very sorry we ever listened to you," Bredan said.

"The problem we had last time," Raimon continued, undaunted, "was that one of us had to buy the voice recorder, and that meant registering by name."

"Technically, we shouldn't have brought it out of the Zone at all," Mikhail said. "Ever since the Sharra uprising at Caer Donn, the *Terranan* have been fanatic about upholding the Compact."

Raimon said, with unwonted seriousness, "If I thought that a simple voice recorder could be used as a weapon, I'd sent it to Zandru's coldest hell before I touched the filthy thing."

Bredan reached out to touch his shoulder, and Raimon relaxed under the pulse of steady love and support that flowed from the brief contact.

The conversation then changed to the latest scandal involving the Golden Cage, Thendara's most notorious brothel. At least in the Darkovan sector, Raimon said. He had heard there was a place in the Terran Zone that could give it some competition.

"The Greek Dancer."

"What does it mean, Greek?" Felix asked.

Mikhail said, "Some ancient *Terranan* custom. Who cares, with dancers like they've got?"

"How come you know so much about it? The man is full of surprises!" Raimon dug an elbow into Mikhail's ribs, prompting a round of sputtering. "Since we've got a personal guide, I think we ought to check this *Terranan* wonder out."

The blood-red sun was just dipping behind the rooftops of the Darkovan sector as the four cadets approached the gate to the Terran Zone. A black-suited guard stepped forward and addressed them in barbarically accented *cahuenga*.

"You can't bring those weapons into the Zone. Either take your swords back home or check them here. And by the way, you boys are minors under Terran law, and therefore subject to curfew. Be back by an hour after sunset, or you'll get reported."

After checking their weapons, the four friends wandered through the gaggle of eating places and small shops gearing up for an evening's business. In comparison with the natural lighting of the old city, the lamps cast eerie, almost supernatural shadows. They paused to inspect some goods prominently displayed on open tables.

"Cheap trade stuff." Raimon sniffed.

Felix bought a stick of spun-synthesugar candy. "This isn't bad."

"Eat enough of that stuff and you'll end up as fat as Alban the Miller—and with as few teeth!" Bredan laughed.

"I think what we want is over this way." Raimon flung an arm around Bredan's shoulders and, ignoring the disapproving stares of the Terran merchants, started down an even more garishly lit avenue.

The Greek Dancer was not difficult to find, even in a mass of buildings of various degrees of taste. A woman leaned from the balcony window, calling lewd suggestions to passers. The Terrans in the street looked up and shouted equally obscene replies, but the Darkovan boys kept their eyes averted. Felix blushed furiously as the blonde, her breasts barely covered by gauze and glitter, offered to relieve him of his virginity.

"C'mon, Felix, it's not as if you'd never been to a brothel

24

before," Raimon said, keeping his voice low so the woman could not hear. The precaution was unnecessary, as she had already turned her attention to more promising prey. "I dragged you there myself for your fifteenth birthday."

"These *Terranan* have no sense of decency," Mikhail said somberly.

"By Aldones, no!" Raimon agreed enthusiastically. "That's what makes them so much fun!"

They elbowed their way into the dimly lit central room and stood for a moment gaping at the decor, especially the glittering wall panels. For Darkovans raised in airy, open buildings of translucent stone, the undulating, closed-in room was momentarily disconcerting, repellent. Then Raimon's eyes dark-adapted and he spied an empty table near a dais that could only be a stage.

A server approached them as soon as they lowered themselves into the sculpted plastic seats. Raimon turned his head to see a length of naked thigh topped by a brief tunic of metallic fabric. Dark eyes gleamed behind a feathered mask and reddened lips curved in an inviting smile.

"What's the matter, cat got your tongue, sweetie?" One hip brushed against his cheek in unmistakable suggestion.

Raimon just stared, for the melodious, honey-sweet voice, like the bulging crotch placed so strategically near his face, was unmistakably male. Raimon was neither a virgin nor a prude, nor was he uncomfortable with the physical expression of love with his *bredu*. But for a man of such dubious morality to approach him in a public place left him momentarily speechless.

Making a noticeable effort to keep his face serious, Bredan told the server, "My friend's tongue seems to be paralyzed. I think spiced wine all around would help."

"We don't have anything that tame, but I can get him a lady's cocktail if you boys aren't up to anything stronger."

Raimon recovered his voice. *A lady's cocktail, indeed!* He searched his memory for the one Terran drink he knew to be suitable for grown men. "Forget that," he snapped. "We'll start with a Callahan Special. All around."

The server glided back toward the bar through the thickening crowd, his hips swaying to an astonishing degree. Bredan said, "Maybe the crazy *Terranan* have an operation like the illegal *emmasca*, only in reverse—instead of becoming neuter, you become both."

The drinks went down like frozen fire, with peculiar aftertaste at the back of the throat. Raimon sipped his as the first act began. A thin woman, who seemed to him to be practically naked to begin with, did an elaborate strip-tease with two feather fans. He noticed that Felix was blushing furiously, his eyes downcast. Finally the dance ended and Mikhail leaned forward to say, "This is only the teaser. It gets better—"

"Mikie, honey-lips! Where you been so long?" Squealing in delight, an unambiguously female server threw her arms around Mikhail's neck and swung her legs onto his lap. The other boys watched, astonished, as she kissed him on the lips. "You boys lookin' for a good time? I'm Kitten, and I'm real friendly!"

"Mikhail, you old—" began Raimon.

"Listen, baby, you seen the show before, you don't need to waste time on it again. Last time you were promised a special treat, much better than the show tonight. What d'ya say?"

After some enthusiastic coaxing from Kitten and not much resistance on the boys' part, they followed her past a layer of rippling wall coverings and down a narrow hallway to a tiny but sumptuously furnished private room. Raimon sat beside Bredan on the low couch that was obviously designed for more than sitting.

"Now you boys just wait a moment and I'll be right back. I been saving this little surprise for Mikie's next visit."

"What's this 'little surprise'?" Raimon asked after she left.

"I don't know. She said she knew something that would 'loosen me up,' whatever that means."

Kitten returned in a few moments with a small black box. "Stygian bloodroot, the real stuff. You never tried anything like it, I guarantee that. No free samples, but you'll never regret it." She named a price that would have left the boys gasping if they had not been so determined to impress her with their worldliness.

Inside the box lay a pile of thin gray threads. Kitten separated one out. "You put it under your tongue," she said. "Don't chew, or we'll be scraping you off of the ceiling. Hold it there and in a few minutes—wowie zowie!"

Gingerly, Raimon picked up a piece. He'd never heard of Stygia, let alone its bloodroot, and he had no idea what to expect. Whatever it did, he reasoned as he placed it beneath his tongue, it was sure to make a great story back at the barracks.

Several things happened at once. Raimon's ears felt as if they'd been shoved in a pot of boiling water, he felt a strong urge to giggle, and there was a brassy honking from the hallway.

Kitten scrambled to her feet. "Oh, shit! We're being raided!"

"*Raided?*" Raimon blinked at her, and then giggled. A strange echo in the room magnified his own laughter.

"Yes, you idiot! It's the narcs!" She slammed the lid of the box shut. "Do you have any idea how illegal this stuff is? I don't know what they'll do to you, but they'll send *me* someplace very boring for a long, long time."

She yanked open the door and disappeared.

"Some friend," muttered Bredan, his speech strangely distorted, almost bubbly. "Leavin' us to take th' blame."

Raimon tried to think, but his vision was beginning to dance with tiny pink butterflies. "We'd better get out of here."

The hallway outside seethed with bodies in various degrees of undress, each apparently trying to go in a different direction. Raimon, first out the door, paused. Someone grabbed his arm, firm but not unfriendly. He recognized the male server who had flirted with him.

"Come on, this is no place for kids." The server pulled him down the hallway to the main room. Raimon reflexively grabbed Bredan's hand, an island of security in a world gone bizarre. The server shoved them toward the back of the dais. "We've got a secret exit— What's the matter with you?"

Mikhail, breathing heavily, stammered, "K-K-Kitten—"

"That bitch! Did she try to pawn spidercrack off on you as bloodroot?"

Raimon nodded as a sudden wave of nausea knotted his stomach.

"You poor innocents. Half the fun and twice the pain, but it won't kill you. Through here—"

Felix and Mikhail dove behind the matte-black curtain, Bredan hesitating only a moment to make sure Raimon was following.

"Freeze where you are! Terran Vice Squad!"

Suddenly the server shouldered his way past and Raimon fell retching to his knees. A moment later he was hauled to his feet by two Terran officers.

For the next hour, as the server had foretold, his stomach and balance centers were in utter revolt, but he managed not to disgrace himself by vomiting. He sat, wrists bound by lightweight force-cuffs, waiting to be formally charged. By the time he had to face questions, the worst had worn off, although waves of nausea still seized him at irregular intervals. It took all of Raimon's guile to keep his jailers from detecting his illness and treating him medically under the emergency care provisions of the Treaty.

"Name?" snapped the grim-looking officer at the desk.

Raimon straightened his shoulders. He was the last of the small group of Darkovan customers to be processed, and his gastrointestinal symptoms were beginning to give way to deep muscle tremors. The last thing he wanted was to appear frightened before this bureaucratic rabbit-horn of a *Terranan*.

"Brendon, Cadet Ensolare...sir."

"Cadet, you are charged with violation of Terran anti-crime law. Consorting with known prostitutes, on the premises where illegal hallucinogens—" Raimon did not even twitch—"were seized, present in an establishment serving alcohol to minors— and I don't doubt that you yourself consumed some. Those are fairly serious charges, enough to get you sent to juvenile rehab if you were in our jurisdiction. But the Darkovan authorities insist we turn you over to them. We will file formal charges against you tomorrow. Until those charges are dismissed by your own superior, or they inform us you have completed whatever penalty they give you, you are not welcome to return to the Terran Zone. Is that clear?"

"Perfectly, sir."

Somehow Raimon managed to make it, escorted, to the border of the Terran Zone and then, unescorted and undiscovered, to the barracks. Bredan was still awake and waiting for him. Raimon knew, without having to kindle a light, that his *bredu* felt no better than he did but with the added burden of worry for his friend.

"What in Zandru's seventh hell happened to you?" Bredan hissed through the darkness. "You were right behind us, but when we came out in the alley, you weren't there. And neither, by the way, was that thrice-bedamned *bre'suin*—"

"He did us all a favor when we got into that mess on our own. But there's no harm done. I was the only one caught and—listen to this, Dan—tomorrow the Terran authorities will be registering formal charges—against *Brendon Ensolare!*"

Raimon felt Bredan's astonished glee like a wave of warmth and he wondered for the hundredth time if one or the other of them might have a trace of *laran*—not enough to show up overtly, but enough to account for the amazing sympathy between them.

Bredan whispered, "What do you suppose Di Asturien will do to him?"

Raimon took off his clothes, stuffed them in the narrow wooden chest at the foot of his bed, and slipped beneath the covers. "Let's just pray it's something he doesn't have to show up in person for."

The next morning, the cadet-master's aide stuck his head into the third-year barracks just as they were finishing dressing for breakfast. "Cadet Ensolare!" He saw the puzzled faces and sniffed. "No one's seen him, eh? Well, you can tell the miscreant that he's assigned double latrine duty for the next month, commander's orders." And then he withdrew.

"You can't say Di Asturien's entirely lacking in a sense of humor," Raimon commented. "He clearly means that those who voluntarily choose the—er, pits, ought to have their wishes granted."

The four friends managed to pick up the extra shifts of latrine duty, so the absence of Cadet Ensolare went unnoticed by the inspecting officers. As the weeks passed, the last residue of the "Stygian bloodroot" faded into a humorous memory, and Raimon's old confidence began to reassert itself.

"It's nearly the end of the Comyn Council season…" Felix began shyly. He stood together with Raimon and Bredan outside the practice fields, waiting for Mikhail to finish his lesson. Having been raised in Kilghard fashion to fight with two knives, Mikhail found the stylized cadet sword work frustrating. When surprised, he would automatically reach for his second blade which, unaccountably, was always somewhere about his person. The arms master was making a concerted effort to teach him decent Lowland technique.

"Too bad, no more honor guard duty," Raimon said lightly, watching Mikhail go through one more timing drill. "Still, it would have been nice to see them in all their splendor at least once, another story to tell the grandkids, right, Bredan?"

Felix took a deep breath and blurted out, "I've been issued an invitation to their closing ball, tomorrow night, and I can bring one guest, and I was wondering if you'd like to attend with me, Raimon…that is, if Bredan doesn't mind."

Raimon and Bredan stared at him. It was one of the longest, and certainly the most astonishing speech they'd even heard him make. Bredan said, "How did you manage an invitation? I didn't think cadets were included in those affairs."

Felix blushed, but less than usual. "You've probably guessed from my hair that there's Comyn blood in my family. My grandmother was a *nedestra* Elhalyn, although usually nobody remembers. I went. I saw Lady Callina about Tower training after I finish this year, and she said I ought to be included."

"A Tower?" Bredan and Raimon exclaimed in unison. "How'd that happen? C'mon, Felix, give!"

The boy looked down at his dusty boots. "I had threshold sickness much worse than my older brother, but everybody said it was because I was so sickly as a child. When I was fourteen, my mother wanted me tested by a *leronis*, but my father said it was more important to make a man of me, so he sent off to the Guards. It wasn't all bad. I mean, I met you two, and Mikhail. But I feel these things, as if I'm a featherdown blown by other people's emotions. I think it would be better to find out how to manage it, even if it turns out to be worthless."

"Aldones!" Raimon breathed. No wonder Felix was always blushing!

"So," said Felix after a long pause, "what do you think?"

"Bredan?"

Bredan grinned and punched Raimon gently in the shoulder. "Go ahead, have a good time. I've got city patrol tomorrow night, anyway."

Raimon sang softly under his breath as he and Felix made their way back, three parts drunk and very pleased with themselves. The ball with its Comyn lords and ladies, officers, and even a crimson-robed Keeper, seemed like a dream. Raimon had worked up enough nerve to dance with several of the young noblewomen, too overwhelmed to notice the details of their gowns that Lanna would certainly question him about. Old

Danvan Hastur himself had been there, along with his young heir. Commander Di Asturien had been gravely polite to both boys, and they had seen Dyan Ardais in the famous sword-dance. All in all, it was a night to tell one's grandchildren.

Felix managed to open the barracks door and they went in. Mikhail, Edric, and a few of the others were clustered around a shielded light. Mikhail looked up, his breath coming in a sob.

"Raimon, thank Aldones you've come."

Something in his voice stung Raimon like ice water, sweeping away the last traces of the wine punch. "What's wrong?"

"It's Bredan," said Edric shakily as Mikhail hid his face in his hands. "I wish I didn't have to be the one to tell you—"

In one movement Raimon shot across the floor, grabbing Edric's shoulders with such force that he lifted the taller boy from the ground. "Damn you! What's happened to Bredan?"

"He's hurt badly. Maybe dying, we don't know yet," said Mikhail.

"There was a fight down by the Golden Cage," Edric cried. "A bunch of damned fools drunk on some stuff they'd gotten illegally in the Terran Zone. Bredan was alone—he tried to separate two of them. One knifed him—under the ribs, I think. They've sent for a healer from the Tower, to try to save him. Rai, I'm so sorry."

Raimon opened hands, barely feeling Edric slump and then catch himself. Images seared his vision, images of darkness and bloodshed. Bredan knifed down in the street, bleeding calling out to him, Bredan lying in a pool of his own blood.

Bredan dying...

"Why—how could he be alone? City patrol is always by pairs."

Mikhail put one hand on his shoulder and said in a low voice, "His assigned second was Brendon Ensolare."

Raimon reeled in shock. There was no Brendon Ensolare to fight at Bredan's side, the difference between life and death, and no Raimon Valdizar to make up the absence, because he had been enjoying himself at the Comyn ball. Bredan had never gotten over feeling personally responsible for Ensolare because of the confusion over his own name, so he hadn't asked for help.

If Dan dies…if he dies it will be my fault. I didn't let him clean up the mistake and I wasn't there when he needed me.

"He's in the infirmary, "Mikhail said gently.

Raimon tore through the door at a run. The infirmarian recognized him and let him in without any questions. He showed him to a small, well-lit room. A young woman wearing a loose white robe, her copper hair spilling over her shoulders, knelt at the side of the bed on which lay a waxen-pale figure, blurred in Raimon's sight.

"Can I go to him?" he whispered.

The infirmarian shook his head, but the woman, without opening her eyes, said, "Yes. You can add your will to live to his."

Raimon sat on the low stool as the head of the bed, looking down at Bredan's face, white and still as if his life fires were already extinguished. Only the slow, almost hesitant rise and fall of his bandaged chest told Raimon that he'd not come too late.

The *leronis* shifted her position, her thin, six-fingered hands outstretched over Bredan's body. "Take his hands," she said. "Let him know you love him."

Bredan's fingers were cold, almost stiff. Raimon willed them to warm with life, with his own life.

Bredan, my brother, my heart, don't leave me. I don't know what I'll do if I lose you because I was so damned cocky.

Tears were running down his face freely now, spilling over their joined hands, but if the *leronis* noticed, she gave no sign.

I thought this whole Ensolare prank was a game, the biggest joke of my career. But I never meant to hurt anyone, never meant it to come to this. If there's a price to pay for my stupidity, let it be me that pays— Oh Avarra, Dark Lady, let it be me and not Bredan!

"Raimon." The voice was low, female, shattering the passion of his agony and guilt. "Raimon, go back and sleep. You can do no more here tonight, and your *bredu* will need all your strength in the morning."

"He will live?"

The *leronis* smiled.

A somber Raimon Valdizar stood before Commander Di Asturien in his private offices, his face still dawn from the weeks of ordeal behind him.

"As you know, sir, Cadet Escobar has still not recovered sufficiently to continue with his duties. The infirmarian suggested that he return home for the rest of the term. I would like permission to accompany him and remain with him until he has regained his health."

"I understand at one time you wished to continue in the Guard as an officer. If you leave now, you'll have to repeat the entire year."

"I—I know that, sir. I'm willing to pay the price."

"Very well, then, as long as you understand the consequences."

"That I do, sir." *Possibly for the first time in my life.* "And sir?"

"Yes…"

"Cadet Ensolare asked to come along, too."

"Cadet Ensolare…ah, yes. That rather brash young man who got himself embroiled with the Terran Vice Squad. I've been meaning to speak to you about him, Cadet Valdizar. You're his friend, maybe you can talk some sense into him. Do you think there's any hope for straightening him out?"

Raimon said with a perfectly straight face, "I think he's learned his lesson, sir."

"Learning a lesson and putting it into action are two completely different matters. Nevertheless, permission is granted to both of you to accompany Cadet Escobar. *Adelandeyo*, go in peace."

Despite the slow pace, Bredan was nearly exhausted by the time his family's small estate came into view. "I need to rest before we take that last stretch," he said, grasping the pommel of his saddle with white-knuckled hands.

"We should have arranged for a travel litter," Raimon said, and sent their hired servant ahead to announce their arrival.

Bredan shook his head, smiling with a trace of his old spirit. "That would have frightened my mother out of her wits for sure. As it is, she'll fuss over me worse than if I were Aldones himself. Believe me, it's better that I arrive sitting up."

They halted their horses in the paved courtyard between the house and the smaller workshops and stables. Bredan's mother, a tiny woman with iron-gray hair, rushed to his side as Raimon helped him to dismount.

"You've come at last—I've been so worried—look at you,

you're as pale as a sheet—Raimon, you take his other arm—
we've got to get him lying down, maybe with some hot wine—
that's good for rebuilding the blood—what a pity Pietro isn't
here to help, but he's gone with your father up toward Gray
Hill, looking for stray stock and the other men are at Armida,
helping with the hay harvest—I can't imagine what your father
will think when he comes home and finds you here already and
him not back to welcome you—there! mind the step," she said
in a single breath.

Bredan looked up at Raimon. *You see what I meant.*

I've got to do something about Brendon Ensolare, Raimon thought
as he watched Bredan's mother bustle about the solarium, tuck-
ing him in with blankets and exhorting him to drink the heated
wine. *Each moment I see Bredan like this I'm reminded how it happened.
I can't forgive myself until the whole game is finished.*

Later in the day, when red shadows were lengthening across
the courtyard and Bredan had sunk into a restful sleep, Raimon
jerked awake from his own dozing at a clatter on the threshold.
He found his way to the front door, where a haggard Pietro
stood, gesturing wildly to Lady Escobar.

"I ran the poor beast half-dead gettin' here, but the Laird
canna hold out for long, not agin those de'ils."

"What's going on? Can I help?" As he drew closer, Raimon
saw deep, welling scratches through the rents in the man's heavy
shirt.

Lady Escobar said, "Catman attack. Since Corresanti, they've
come farther south, but usually toward Alton lands, so we
thought we were safe. My husband's trapped in one of the Gray
Hill caves. There's only us women and one old man to send,
since Pietro's wounded." Gone was the fussiness, replaced by a
quiet fatality.

"I'll go. Bredan showed me where it was on my last visit."

She looked at him, her gaze measuring. "You don't owe us this."

"Your son and I are *bredin*," he said, using the inflection that meant "sworn brother."

Minutes later Raimon was pounding up the trail, his sword slung across his back. It was almost dark when he pulled his lathered horse to a halt, scanning the fractured granite of Gray Hill. The caves lay along the east side along the switchbacks that crossed its creviced face. He saw the glimmer of torchlight aloft and spurred his panting mount forward.

Two catmen, armed with curved Dry Town blades, held the sloping, pebble-strewn apron at the cave's entrance. They whirled, alert and ready even before Raimon leapt from the saddle, sworn in his hand. The horse, snorting in outrage, bolted back down the trail.

One catman uttered unintelligible curses and hurled itself through the air toward Raimon. He parried its blade, but it tossed the sword away and sank its extended claws into his shoulder.

Raimon staggered under the sudden impact of the catman's weight, twisting aside so that the deadly hind claws swept through empty air instead of his own belly. He fell to one knee as the creature spun away with inhuman agility to renew its attack.

Suddenly the catman's battle cry turned to a scream of panic as it clawed frantically at the loose, sliding rock. The apron of pebble and weather-crazed stone tumbled free in a miniature avalanche. The catman went with it, flailing and yowling, but unable to regain its footing on the treacherous slide. It sank from view as its voice fell silent, and no further sign of life came from below.

The rock beneath Raimon's knee began to give way with a sickening wrench. He scrambled to his feet on what was left of the narrow trail, coughing on the acrid dust. The remaining catman crouched before him, blade raised and glimmering in the failing light. It sank into a fighting stance, blocking the entrance with clear malice. Just inside the cave lay a pile of dark, unmoving bodies, evidence of Escobar's defense.

"Lord Escobar! Are you all right?"

"Aye, for the moment, but m'leg's broken."

"There's only one of the things lef—"

With a murderous growl, the catman shot forward, aiming not for Raimon but for the remnants of the trail at his feet. A quick slash sent Raimon jumping backward, and the catman dug its sword tip into the loose stone and pushed outward. A flurry of rock tumbled down the hillside.

Sliding his feet to feel his way, Raimon inched forward. If only he could get close enough to reach the cursed thing before it pried loose so much of the trail that he either suffered the same fate as the first catman or else was cut off completely from the cave. The catman, seeing his intention, jumped forward in last, desperate assault.

Raimon met the attack, his muscles flowing into the patterns Timas Wellsmith had drilled into him. Without thinking, he parried, disengaged, and thrust clean through the catman's guard. A scream and sudden wavering of the curved blade told Raimon his own sword had found its mark. He was fighting by instinct and feel rather than sight now, could barely see his opponent in the near darkness. Part of him wanted to break off this impossible battle and go running back down the trail to safety. Any moment now, he might go tumbling down the hillside to break his neck on the rock fall, or miss a lightning thrust of the catman's black and die in a pool of his own blood.

But Bredan had very nearly died that way…

Raimon brought himself up with a start, realizing that the catman had suddenly disappeared. He stepped forward, expecting a renewed attack at any moment. The torchlight from the cave guided him, for a moment illuminating the entire arch of the entrance. Then he spied the catman in silhouette, clinging to the upper wall. It was using its sword as a lever, the point thrust deep into the crevice.

Raimon's blade sped upward toward its unguarded belly, but the catman twisted and lost its footing in a shower of granite slivers. Raimon flinched, raising his free hand to protect his eyes. The catman's hind legs churned madly against the stone face, fighting desperately for purchase while its weight fell against the sword.

Raimon slashed upward again. This time his blade met living flesh. He felt it glance off bone and jerk forward, almost out of his grip.

A sudden *crack!* brought another shower of fresh rock as the catman loosened its grip upon the sword and jumped free. A huge piece of stone from the overhang came hurling outward. It caught the catman even as it leapt for the entrance, and disappeared downslope.

Raimon watched in horror as the entire outside face of rock began to break up. Without thinking, he dropped his sword, whirled, and dove into the cave. Lord Escobar had hauled himself upright, standing on one leg. His face was set and grim in the dying torchlight. He hobbled forward as Raimon shouted, "Let's go!" and hooked his arm under the old man's shoulder.

In the few seconds it took them to reach the entrance, more

stone had fallen, almost closing the passageway. Lord Escobar hesitated in the fall of dust and rock. "No use, lad."

"It's our only chance!" Raimon cried. He couldn't give up, not with Bredan's father depending upon him, not even if he died in the attempt. He shoved the old man bodily through the rapidly disappearing opening.

Loose rock pelted them and Raimon ducked, trying to shield the old man. A chunk of granite struck Escobar on the side of the head with a sickening *whap!* and suddenly he went limp in Raimon's arms.

Raimon did not feel the shower of stones battering his own body or the shrieking pain in his arms as he hauled Escobar's inert body to the last strip of clear trail. He had only a moment to sling the old man across his shoulders before that, too, began to slide under his feet. Half-running, half-scrambling, he somehow kept going down the nightmare trail until he reached level ground.

Gently Raimon laid the old man down on a patch of grass. His breathing was shallow and regular, but he did not rouse when Raimon, using strips cut from his own under tunic, lashed two pieces of fallen wood to his leg to brace the fracture. Then came a more difficult decision, for even though further movement might worsen Escobar's head injury, Raimon could not leave him, not with the night chill already seeping into his bones and possibly more catmen prowling the darkness.

Dredging his memory for the details of Gabriel Lanart-Hastur's tales of mountain rescues, Raimon used what was left of his shirt to tie Lord Escobar so that he could carry him more easily. How he made it through the night, staggering up one hill and stumbling down again, he never knew. He stopped counting the rest stops he was forced to take when he simply could not

41

make his legs move any farther.

Some hours past dawn, Raimon's ordeal came to an end. Pietro met them along the trail with whoops of joy and an extra saddled horse. The return of Raimon's riderless mount had caused near panic, and he had been sent to see if anything could be done before sending to Armida for help.

Bredan and his mother rushed forward to meet them before they set foot in the courtyard. Clearly, neither had slept all night. As the injured lord was put to bed, his fracture set and other wounds tended, Raimon sat silently by the fire, holding Bredan's hands with one hand and a cup of hot wine with the other. He had eaten and bathed, and the scratches on his shoulder were bandaged, but he was far from sleep.

"Raimon, I cannot thank you enough. You—you saved his life, you know." Lady Escobar stood in the doorway, her face careworn but radiant. "You have proven yourself a true hero—"

"He's going to be all right?" Raimon asked, ignoring the gratitude in her eyes.

"Evanda willing, he will outlive us all. His skull is not broken, only stunned. He is awake now and wants to thank you himself."

"It was a brave rescue ye did, lad," said Bredan's father. His dark eyes sparkled beneath his bandaged forehead, although he seemed a little confused about what happened to him.

"No, it wasn't." Raimon replied in a low voice. "I mean, it wasn't me."

He took a deep breath and said again, "It wasn't me that saved you. It was Brendon Ensolare, a fellow cadet, a friend to Bredan and me. He was delayed on the trail, but he followed me to Gray Hill. He fought at my side against the catmen and carried you out when I couldn't get past the cave entrance. But he was caught in the landslide, buried in the rock. He died saving us both."

For a fleeting moment, Bredan looked confused, and then he said, "That would be just like Ensolare, to show up when he's least expected. But unlike you, Raimon, to give away the credit when you might be acclaimed as a hero. You always loved being the center of attention."

"I—I can't accept what I don't deserve," Raimon stammered. "The important thing is that your father is alive and recovering."

"I am pleased that my son had such a friend. We must send word to his family," said Lord Escobar.

"I don't think he has a family outside of the Guards, Father," Bredan said.

"Sad, but he will not be forgotten," the old man commented, and drifted into sleep.

Raimon Valdizar stood in the great hall of Comyn Castle, waiting for the formal ceremonies to open the next year's season. He was old for a third-year cadet now, and he could tell by their expressions that the younger boys considered him stodgy. He didn't care, for at his side stood Bredan Escobar, alive and well.

Domenic Di Asturien stepped forward to begin the ceremony, just as he had on that fateful day a year ago. But this time there would be no Brendon Ensolare on the roll.

Raimon had visited Di Asturien in private upon his return to Thendara to inform the commander of the heroic death of Cadet Ensolare.

"He died bravely, a credit to the Guards. Lord Escobar sent this letter of commendation."

The old soldier took the note. "We'll miss the lad, but perhaps it's all for the best." And then, suddenly, "Do you like nuts, Cadet Valdizar?"

"Sir!"

"Nuts. Ambernuts, hazels, pitchoos."

"Y-yes, sir."

"The principle thing about nuts, Valdizar, is that each requires a different technique. Pitchoos, now, they're covered with such a delicate skin that even a fingernail can mar the fruit inside. Barknuts are sweet enough, and easy to crack with a common nutcracker. But ambernuts are a different matter. To get at the meat, you have to throw them in a fire. Nothing less will break through that hard shell, but when you're done, you have the best eating of all. Do you understand me?"

"I think so, sir." *Aldones, he must have known all along...*

"Then run along. I'll see you and your friend at call-over. And, Cadet Valdizar... Don't either of you forget your names this time. I don't think the Guard could survive another season like the last one."

"Acurrhir Todo; Nada Perdonad"

A Tale of the Hundred Kingdoms

The great hall of Avery stank of smoldering clingfire, dust, and sweat. Duncan Inverness stood in a corner with the junior officers and aides, watching the formal surrender and wondering, *Why did Father summon me from Arilinn just to watch a few beaten men kiss his sword? He was quick enough to send me there when he wanted to get me out of the way.*

Many of the defending forces, including Lord Avery's chief sorcerer, lay buried in the rubble of the once-magnificent eastern tower, and more had fallen to the swords of the Inverness troops. Duncan kept his face carefully neutral as he watched his father, resplendent in crimson and gold silk over his battered mail, take his seat in the great carved throne.

Gherig, Lord of Inverness and half a dozen other kingdoms, laid his naked sword across his knees, stroked the red-and-silver beard that was his sole personal vanity, and ordered the prisoners to be brought before him. Behind one shoulder towered his elder son and heir, Rafael, and behind the other, the foremost *laranzu* of his circle. Rafael, his face streaked with smoke and dried blood from his last berserker charge at the city gates, looked out over the mass of prisoners with eyes as cold as a hawk's.

Watching his older brother, Duncan shivered with longing for Arilinn Tower and its people, who had taught him useful work and valued him for it. Here he was nothing more than an encumbrance, with little knowledge and less taste for warfare. The boys his own age stood in awe of him because of the accident of his birth, while his once-adored brother had become a blood-spattered stranger, as quick to strangle an enemy with his bare hands as spit at him.

I'm only here because Father thought I was growing too soft in the Tower and a campaign might make me more like Rafe, Duncan realized. *Easier to put a banshee chick back into its shell...*

Two burly Inverness men-at-arms dragged up Mikhail, Lord Avery, reputed to be a ruthless administrator but obviously no war-leader. With the death of his *laranzu*, his effective resistance had evaporated, and now all that remained of his psychic defenses were a few women of minor talent huddled in the far corner with the ladies' maids.

Avery himself was a lumpy potato of a man, his waxen face marked by spots of hectic color on each round cheek. He wore a suit of ornamental armor that was too small for him. He reminded Duncan of a boy he'd known his first year at Arilinn, who'd bullied the small children until he learned to master his own fears.

"Always look beyond the obvious," his Keeper had repeated. "Nothing, not physical appearance nor even *laran* is ever truly as we first assume it to be." If Beral was a coward underneath his boasting, what lay beneath Mikhail's mask of softness?

Gherig adopted his sternest expression as he listened to the ritual words that completed the surrender. Leaning heavily on his guards, Mikhail knelt and kissed the hilt of the Inverness sword. Then the remainder of the Avery family—a pale wraith of a wife with a tight, resentful mouth, two tear-stained, pimple-faced daughters, and a boy well on his way to becoming a duplicate of his father—came forward one by one to swear fealty to their new lord.

Gherig probably wouldn't even bother to execute them, Duncan thought, and remembered the stories of his father's first conquest, a gray wolf of a MacAldran who fought like Zandru's demons to the very last. Given half a chance, he'd have risen again, so there was no choice but to give him a quick and honorable death. As for the Averys, Gherig would only exile them, thinking them incapable of a serious threat.

The courtiers, minor nobles who'd stood by Avery from traditional loyalty, came forward next. Gherig arranged for hostages from their families and let them go with their lives, and gave them only modest fines. Duncan sensed their relieved thoughts: *Lord Avery would have executed us and confiscated our estates. All those stories about his hothead son slicing men to shreds for the sheer bloodlust were just soldier's tales. Inverness is a fair man.*

The *coridom* had been killed in the fall of the eastern tower, but his assistant waited with the rest of the household staff. Duncan was stunned by the sheer physical beauty of the young man who stepped forward to kneel at Gherig's feet. Slight but not girlish, he carried himself with a sword-dancer's grace. His red-tinted hair curled over his shoulders, just a trace long for a boy his age, and when he looked up, Duncan got a clear view of the wide, wine-dark eyes, the fine line of the beardless jaw, the full, sensitive lips. There was something both reserved and

47

provocative about the way he stood before his new lord. Duncan considered this, together with the too-long curls—had he been Mikhail's catamite, and did that account for the perennial resentment engraved upon Lady Avery's prune-like mouth? Too obvious, always question the obvious.

Gherig gestured Duncan forward and ordered the boy, Anndra, to familiarize him with the records. Duncan remained on the dais, standing behind Rafael, bemused at this sudden turn of events. It hadn't occurred to him that his father had any actual use for him on this campaign.

Gherig dispensed with the Avery captains, again pardoning them with affordable fines, and sent Rafael down to supervise the cleansing of the dungeons. Rafael's men brought out the usual rabble, a handful of flea-ridden beggars squinting in the light. The first one cowered at Gherig's feet and confessed to stealing a pig to feed his family.

"Free him," Gherig commanded. Duncan smiled as a ripple of astonishment spread through the assembly. By morning, tales of the new lord's mercy would be all over the city, and he'd have a far easier time keeping order.

Gherig repeated this verdict for the other prisoners, pathetic creatures accused of relatively minor crimes. After they were gone, scuttling to whatever holes would take them, Rafael said, "*Vai dom*, there's one more prisoner, a special case."

Gherig raised an inquiring eyebrow. Rafael gestured to the far end of the hall where a slender, white-haired woman sagged between two guards. Her thin arms, scratched and filthy, shone through the tatters of her robes, and her feet were bare despite the chill. Beneath the tangle of her unbound hair, little of her face could be seen.

"We found her in a cell well away from the others. Heavily

chained and guarded by this…"

Rafael took a small box of wood and metal from one of his aides and handed it to Gherig. Duncan had never seen anything like it, nor felt anything like the disturbing vibration that left him nauseated and disoriented. Yet Gherig, turning the box over in his hands, showed no sign of discomfort.

"*Vai dom*," murmured the *laranzu* at Gherig's side.

"Yes, Aldric, what is it?"

The gray-eyed sorcerer took the box from Gherig. His usually impassive face, framed in a severely cut red beard, was ashen, almost shocky. He touched a panel on the side of the box, and Duncan's senses cleared abruptly. "This is a telepathic damper, and nothing to trifle with."

"A telepathic— What sort of prisoner needs that to guard her?"

Gravely, Aldric approached the woman and stood for a long moment, scanning her for the depth and quality of her *laran*. "She has some talent, but it's deeply buried. I doubt she has more than rudimentary empathy, possibly some clairvoyance. Nothing that could constitute a military threat. You could have her tested to be sure."

"No, I trust your judgment, Aldric," Gherig replied. "Why would he waste this device to guard one harmless woman? Avery! What's the meaning of this?"

The conquered lord staggered forward, and this time there was no disguising the terror on his corpulent features. He fell to his knees before Gherig. "Lord Inverness! *Vai dom!* I beg of you, don't free her! You have no idea of the consequences—"

"What consequences? What did this poor old woman ever do to you?"

"She is an Aldaran Assassin, discovered by my circle—"

An Aldaran Assassin! Part myth, part conjecture, Duncan had heard them discussed in the Tower. Although outwardly ordinary, they were psychically implanted with suicidally fanatic killer conditioning, knowledge of their targets so deeply buried that no *laran* probe could uncover it. They behaved as law-abiding folk until the trigger code was given by their employer, when their conditioning went into operation. They were said to be infallible, a product of the most advanced *laran* technology, which is why they were attributed to the notorious Aldaran clan. Most of what was known was conjecture only, for no living Assassin had ever been interrogated. Mikhail must have kept her alive in the hope he could break her conditioning and force her to serve him, even against her own patron.

"Aldaran Assassins are a myth, a bogey story invented to frighten children," Gherig sneered. "We are not such cowards as to give credence to these tales. Yet she may not be so harmless after all. Give her a hot meal and put her back in her cell, well guarded. I'll decide what to do with her tomorrow morning. Here," Gherig tossed the damper box back to his *laranzu.* "Burn it, keep it, I don't care so long as I never see the thing again. Let's have wine and harpers to sing of how my son charged the Avery gates!"

But the victory feast was short, as if all savor had gone out of the rich stores. Gherig went to bed early, and alone.

And was found alone the next morning by his aides, stone cold. Careful examination of his room revealed a previously hidden passageway, its thick cobwebs recently disturbed. Rafael's first act upon assuming command was to personally hang all the Averys from the battlements, pimple-faced daughters and all.

They laid the body in the cold cellar until preparations could be made for a proper funeral. While the guards paced outside, Duncan sat alone in the ice-rimmed chamber. Something niggled at the back of his senses, something that didn't taste right. He drew his cloak around him and looked down at the stone butcher's slab on which his father lay. Aldric and the chief physician both said that he'd died from a single dagger thrust, the blade slipping between the ribs to pierce the heart.

"If the murderer wasn't actually one of the Averys," Rafael had insisted when Duncan pointed out that the family had been under lock and guard all night, "then it was one of their agents or sympathizers. Either way, the Averys were responsible for Father's death, and now I've put an end to them."

Duncan slipped off his gloves and opened the front of Gherig's heavily embroidered tunic. The old man's face looked haggard, as if death had not yet brought him any respite from the stresses of his lifetime. Duncan parted the *linex* undershirt to expose the wound. The lips gaped a little, showing dark flesh beneath, but all traces of the bleeding had been washed away.

Shivering in the cold but unwilling to sacrifice the sensitivity of his bare hands, Duncan spread his fingers wide over the cut. Closing his eyes, searching with all his Tower-trained *laran*, he sensed the life-ashes of bone and muscle cells, the nerves lying like shriveled cords where once they sparked with energy. No hint of Gherig's spirit remained in the half-frozen husk. There was no trace of any misuse of *laran*, and after long moments of struggle, Duncan opened his eyes again. Why had he expected to find anything? Aldric, a potent *laranzu* skilled in matters of bloodshed, had declared the crime to be ordinary murder.

He gazed at his father's face, wondering why he felt so little grief. The grizzled veteran before him was a stranger. Duncan remembered a younger man, his red beard innocent of gray, who used to play with him by the fountain courtyard at Inverness, but never as long or as frequently as he craved, a man whose later visits were no more than a stormy voice brushing him aside and calling for Rafael's sword practice.

You gave me a place at Arilinn, even though you didn't know what it would mean to me. I owe you for this, at least, Duncan thought. *Rafe may think he's already caught and punished your killer, but I don't believe it.*

Duncan stepped into the street beyond the castle, his bodyguard at his heels. He paused for a moment, watching the Inverness captains organize repair crews and direct carts of hoarded grain for distribution to the townsfolk. Even here in the city, Duncan doubted there were many who'd want to bring back Mikhail's reign.

Unless, Duncan thought as he turned down a side street punctuated by entertainment establishments of the less proper sort, unless that Assassin was involved. Rafael had released her after the guards swore she'd been in her cell all night. An apple-cheeked scullery maid, perhaps hoping for a liaison with the younger son, told Duncan where she'd gone, an inn near the town gates. The innkeeper showed him to the private room where the white-haired woman known only as Mhari sat finishing her midday meal.

Duncan left his bodyguard at the door and sat down facing her. The woman glanced up, and he saw that she was not old. Her eyes were green like the sea, and she looked at him directly, like a Comynara of the Towers or a bold Hellers girl. She wore traveling garb, full skirts and a wool-lined leather jacket. "I'm sorry about your father, *vai dom.*"

At her words, something broke inside Duncan, and his mouth flooded with bitterness. "Did you then repay him with a knife in his heart?"

He knew from the flicker of horror in Mhari's response that she had not. She'd been in the city well before the battle, and had spent most of it in Mikhail's dungeons. She must have been hired before Gherig's victory was certain. Duncan waved aside her denial, saying, "Lord Avery thought you were an Aldaran Assassin. Are you?"

Mhari sopped up the last on her thin soup with a hunk of hard bread. "If so, I have not killed anyone here," she said carefully, "so you cannot hold me accountable on that score. With both lords dead, the new and the old, all deals would be off, anyway."

"Who was your patron; can you at least tell me that?"

She shoved the empty wooden bowl and spoon across the table. "Even if I knew, which I don't, I wouldn't. What assistance could I offer if I let anybody know who hired me?"

"I'm not anybody. I'm Gherig's son, and he could've had your throat slit."

"I owe you for that, so I'll make a bargain in exchange for safe passage out of the city." Duncan nodded, knowing he could easily arrange this. "The password was, *'Acurrhir todo, nada perdonad'.*"

"Remember everything, forget nothing," Duncan mentally translated the ancient words. A rather vindictive choice of phrase. He said, "Assuming Mikhail was right and he was your target, who hated him enough to kill him?"

"Who didn't?" Mhari replied with some heat. "You saw his

courtiers and how little love they bore him. Ask young Anndra Dell'Breya what happened to his family."

"Anndra? The *coridom's* assistant?"

"His people ruled here until about ten years ago. Mikhail took the castle in a sneak attack, put the old lord and lady and the two older sons to the sword, and took the daughter as *barragana*. She was only fourteen when she died in childbirth. What hold he's had over the boy is anyone's guess, but one look at him and you can imagine."

"How do you know all this?"

This time Mhari laughed in his face. "Liege lords come and go, but somebody's got to scrub the pots. Good luck to you, Gherig's-son. I don't envy you the scorpion-ant's nest you've stumbled into."

Mhari's words came back to Duncan several days later, as he sat in the *coridom's* office, going over the books with Anndra. The room was plain, well-lit, sparse in comfort but thick with years of leather-bound books. Anndra spread the current records out on the table, explaining everything in a dry, precise voice. The system was simple, but the required detail suggested an almost pathological preoccupation on Mikhail's part with every grain that was his, rightfully or not. Duncan glanced over the city ledgers, the records of fines levied and paid, momentarily stunned by their harshness,

"This will change," he muttered, "this pointless greed."

There was a firm tap on the door and the junior officer who served as Duncan's bodyguard stepped in, "Your pardon for the interruption, Lord Duncan, but I don't think this should wait."

"What is it, Stefan?" Duncan got up and drew the man aside into a corner.

"You sent me with a packet of documents for the woman named Mhari, staying at the Salamander Inn, but when I got there, they told me she'd been found dead this morning. A knife through the heart, much as the old lord died. I myself saw the body."

As the old lord died. Had Gherig and Mhari been killed by the same person? Numbly Duncan replied, "You did right to tell me. Make sure the Lord Inverness also hears of this."

As he turned back toward the table, Duncan caught a glimpse of Anndra's momentarily unguarded expression. Instead of the smooth mask of deference, the boy's face flushed livid with some overwhelming, unreadable emotion. Anndra's eyes burned like two black flames, his lips drawn tight across his teeth as if to throttle a scream, his face first flushed, then deathly pale.

In compassion, Duncan brushed his fingers along the boy's shoulder, an unusual touch for one Tower-trained. Something inside the Dell'Breya boy exploded like a clingfire missile and he cried aloud, his eyes no longer human but miniature firestorms.

Images flooded through the widening cracks in Anndra's *laran* barriers, blotting out the quiet, sunlit room. For a moment Duncan was Anndra as an exquisitely sensitive child, his talent just budding with adolescence, only to be shredded by the dying agonies of his parents' fully developed minds...a girl's face—*Lirelle!*—dark-lashed eyes the color of rainwater, a dimple at the corner of her laughing mouth...his hands lashed behind his back so tightly his shoulders almost dislocated, the flushed pudgy face so close to his that he gagged on the wine-soaked breath, soft hands patting him, lips pressed against his teeth, the stinking tongue filling his mouth as Mikhail tore his clothes away as he fled, fled into darkness lit only by Lirelle's scream...

Duncan scrambled backward, his heart pounding. His breath came ragged but no blast scorched his lungs or crisped his skin. The illusion disappeared as quickly as it had come. He took his seat, considering his next step. The boy's traumatically-induced *laran* barriers were rapidly shredding, and he ought to have skilled Tower help before he broke down entirely. The depth of his pain and fury, still unhealed after all these years, dismayed Duncan.

The awkward silence had gone on overlong. Anndra, his eyes lowered under silky lashes, murmured, "Did you wish to see the household accounts now, Lord Duncan?"

"Thank you, no, you may return to your other duties. I want to review what you've already shown me."

As soon as Anndra gracefully bowed out of the room, Duncan jumped up and began pacing, as if he could walk off the questions that roiled within him. Anndra clearly hated Mikhail, but he was not the only one. Then why was it Gherig and not Mikhail who'd died with a dagger in his heart, Gherig who'd freed them? The obvious conclusion was that there was no relationship between the two facts, but Duncan could not escape the question: What did Mikhail's death have to do with Gherig's murder?

To distract his thoughts from this frustrating and unprofitable trend, Duncan scanned the neatly shelved ledgers, going back through the decade of Mikhail's reign. He took down a volume of tax rolls from eight years ago and opened it. The ink was still dark on the fine vellum, the handwriting meticulous, and the contents very much the same as the record Anndra had shown him. Back toward the corner farthest from the windows the volumes were dusty, their leather spines showing age but not wear. From the time of the Dell'Breyas?

Duncan thought of how the records of Mikhail's reign revealed his personality. Perhaps there was something to be gained by learning more of the preceding lord. He picked a book from the top shelf and opened it, the pages crackling as he turned to the inscription. Dates, contents...

And there on the title page, a coat-of-arms in colors just beginning to muddy with time. He held it up to the window light to be sure of the motto in tiny, perfectly calligraphed letters across the family crest:

Acurrhir todo; Nada perdonad.

The next day, Duncan sat alone in the *coridom's* office, the preliminary household inventories lying unread on the table before him. Anndra was already late, which was unlike him, but Duncan was just as glad to have a little time to sort out his thoughts. He knew now why Gherig had died, and who'd killed him, but he couldn't see a way to make Rafael listen to him, and if by some miracle he did, he'd never be free to return to the Tower again. He'd be chained to his brother's side as surely as if they were linked by living flesh. Already he pined for Arilinn, like an uprooted *kireseth* blossom withering on the stalk.

Hi thoughts came to an abrupt halt as he heard a faint knocking at the door, so timid, as if scarcely daring to be heard. He got up and opened the door. The girl standing outside was the same one who'd told him where Mhari had gone, and she'd clearly been crying.

"What's wrong, *chiya?*" Duncan asked, unexpectedly affected by her inflamed eyes and trembling mouth.

"Oh, Master Duncan, it's the new lord, he—he's taken Master Anndra, he'll—he says he'll hang him! Oh, please, can't you do something?"

"Where is he now?"

"South tower."

Duncan raced past her, pounding down the stone-floored corridor, up a flight of stairs, past several sets of astonished guards, up more steps. He burst onto the parapet, where Rafael had a hangman's noose around young Anndra's neck and was about to hurl him bodily over the battlement. Duncan had barely enough breath left to shout a warning.

Rafael paid him no heed, pausing only when Duncan grabbed one burly arm and yanked him with all his might. Anndra, his hands bound behind him, was halfway over the slitted gray stones. Duncan pulled him back to the balcony.

"What're you doing?" growled the new Lord Inverness, his mouth distorted into a grimace.

"What are you doing?" Duncan retorted. "Hanging this—"

"This bloody-handed murderer, that's what! He's the one who slaughtered Gherig. My man found the dagger in his possession—Aldric swears it's the right one. Let go of me, you young pup!"

"You brainless *cralmac*!" Duncan screamed with enough genuine outrage to penetrate his brother's killing haze. "You've already killed Mikhail Avery without stopping to think if you had the right man! Are you going to make the same mistake all over again?"

The flush on Rafael's face cleared a little. He loosened his grip, and Anndra dropped to the floor. Duncan caught the expression on the boy's face before his head fell forward, a look of such agony that it tore at his heart. "Rafe," he said, "Anndra *hated* Mikhail."

"So Father thought—trusted him—let him loose in the castle—free to come and go—to sneak around wherever he pleased."

"Won't you at least listen before you hang another man for all the wrong reasons? Rafe, you've got to hear his story before you judge him."

Finally Rafael nodded and signaled the guards at the end of the balcony to follow them to his private chambers. Gherig had originally selected this suite of simply furnished rooms instead of Mikhail's opulent quarters.

Rafael took the central seat, a plain piece ample enough for his bulk. Duncan removed the ropes from Anndra and pushed him into one of the other chairs. The boy sat like a waxen image, his dark eyes lifeless, and no trace of his powerful *laran* flickering past his desperately tight barriers.

"You'd better had a good explanation for this," Rafael muttered. "I'll grant you this cub hated Mikhail, but why would he kill Gherig, who freed him?"

"I didn't say he killed him."

"I told you we found the dagger in his things, and damned careless he was with hiding it, too. Aldric says it was the one used to kill Father as well as that woman from the dungeons."

"I know."

"If Anndra didn't kill Father, who did?"

Duncan took a deep breath. This was the moment when all might be lost. He kept his voice calm, using every scrap of Tower discipline, forcing the ring of truth into his words.

"You did."

"I?" Rafael leapt to his feet, shouting, "I? I loved Gherig

more than I love my own life! How dare you accuse me, you treacherous—"

It took all of Duncan's Tower training to stand immobile as Rafael encircled his throat with his hands, hands that had run with hot blood on countless battlefields.

I cannot fight him strength against strength. Either he will remember the love we shared as brothers, or I will die.

After an agonizing moment when Duncan's vision swam red and then gray, Rafael released him with a savage jerk and threw himself back in his chair, obviously shaken. "Give me one good reason why I should not hang you at the side of this traitor."

"You were right, Rafe. Anndra did hate Mikhail, hated him so much he managed to raise the price of an Aldaran Assassin. Mikhail guessed correctly; he was the target, although he wasn't sure who hired her. But consider this--"

Duncan began pacing, moving between his brother and Anndra. The boy sat hunched over, his downcast eyes unreadable.

"Consider this," he repeated, praying for strength, "the Assassin was somehow discovered by Mikhail, imprisoned, even guarded by a telepathic damper lest her trigger phrase be delivered psychically. Anndra must have been desperate, having come so close, only to be blocked. Then Avery fell, and he saw his new lord—just, merciful. So merciful he would not even execute Mikhail, only exile him beyond Anndra's reach. What was he to do then—allow the monster who had slaughtered his family to go on living? The monster that turned his sister into a *barragana* when she was still a child, who—"

Anndra was weeping silently now. His dark hair his face, but his agony shrieked like a banshee through Duncan's mind.

Duncan went on. "He couldn't get past our guards to kill

Mikhail himself, and he couldn't reach the Assassin, so he had to get someone else to do it for him."

"I killed Mikhail."

"Exactly."

Rafael ran his big hands over his face, his cheeks gone suddenly bloodless. "He killed Father so that I would blame Mikhail—*I* would be his Assassin. I never stopped to think…"

Duncan leaned over his brother's shoulder, hating what he must do, knowing that he had no choice. "Even here, everyone knew your reputation—berserk in battle, hot-tempered. The harpers sang of it that first night for the victory feast, don't you remember? You used to boast that you were like a blade in Father's hands, that he did the thinking for both of you."

"What of it?" Rafael shot back. "I was not the one to creep into Father's bedchamber, I did not slip a dagger into his heart—this *bre'suin* did, and he will hang for it!" He lurched forward as if to throttle the boy then and there. Anndra's shoulders sagged a little farther, and Duncan knew that he would do nothing to defend himself, not even a single word of explanation.

Quickly he continued, "Had you been a man who thinks before he kills, a man who considers and questions the obvious—a leader like Gherig—then he could never have used you, and Gherig would not have had to die for his vengeance."

"That's true enough," Rafael admitted, subsiding, "and I will be the one to pay for it. But I can't let Father's murder go unavenged."

"Don't you think he's been punished enough—" Duncan began, but Anndra cut him off.

"How dare you offer me compassion? When I was innocent and had done no wrong, Mikhail destroyed everyone I loved, and then would not let me follow them. He kept me alive, at his side, in his bed, telling me how merciful he was!" His voice came in ragged gasps as the fire raging behind his eyes threatened to engulf his fragile sanity. "Now that I have blood-guilt on my hands, I don't deserve to live!"

"The real blame for Gherig's murder lies with Mikhail, not this tormented child," Duncan said quietly, "I wondered at first why Mhari was killed when she hadn't fulfilled her mission. Anndra couldn't take the chance she'd told me something vital, just as he couldn't wait until Mikhail was in exile to track him down. So he used the password to get close enough to kill her, and that started me thinking of the connection between Mikhail's death and Father's."

Rafael nodded. "All he had to do was nothing, and his place here would have been secure. No one would question him going about his duties. The way the dagger fell out of his cloak, he wanted to be caught. But I still don't know what I should do with him. Even if he did have good cause, I can't turn him loose."

"Send him to Arilinn for healing. He has *laran* of great power, which he has not used against us, not even in his own defense. He may yet learn to use it for good. I think he at least deserves a chance to make up for the wrong he's done."

Rafael ran one hand through his hair as his face slowly regained its normal color. *He's not a stupid man*, Duncan thought, *or a cruel one, but only one who has stood too long in his father's shadow.* "Arilinn, then, but you'd better get him out of my sight before I change my mind. I suppose you'll want to scuttle back there with him."

Duncan drew a surprised breath. He'd assumed he'd have to stay on at Avery, acting as *coridom* and helping his brother make the right choices from not on. He saw how close he'd come to making a terrible mistake in offering to be his brother's counselor. "Would you really want me here, looking over your shoulder? Even if you didn't come to resent me, you'd never feel free to make your own decisions, as you must."

Rafael got up and drew Duncan into a brother's embrace. Only Duncan's *laran* senses told him how close the big man was to tears. "Bare is brotherless back."

His mouth muffled against the crimson leather of Rafael's tunic, Duncan said, "Keep Inverness and Avery, rule them well." *And let me return to my own place, my own inheritance.*

Gripping Duncan's shoulders in fingers of steel, Rafael drew back, "Where did you learn wisdom so young? Is this what they taught you at Arilinn Tower?"

"Only to look beyond the obvious, even in the human heart."

A Midsummer Night's Gift

M idsummer Eve was not, reflected Gavriela n'ha Alys, the most favorable time to be crossing the dense forests bordering the Venza River. It was warm, almost hushed beneath the canopy of green, even in the occasional wildflower-dotted glades where the massive resin trees had burned like torches and their successors were not yet fully grown. The three Renunciates seemed to be the only creatures moving in the forest, except for an occasional far-off bird. There was no sign of trailmen, who could be dangerous to such a small party. Fiona, their guide, had chosen a route far from their territory, to avoid any chance encounter.

If she'd had her way, Gavi would have waited a few days, but Fiona and Maire had jobs in Hali, and Gavi had learned from painful experience never to travel alone. She'd known Fiona slightly at the Thendara Guildhouse, where she'd studied midwifery, but now wished she'd never set eyes on the woman. Since they'd left Rosario, she and Maire kept teasing Gavi about missing the Midsummer Festival. Sometimes it was with the condescending tone of adults scolding a child greedy for unwholesome sweets, but sometimes their laughing barbs stung more than either of them guessed.

Gavi set her lips together and brushed away the drops of sweat that had gathered on her lank auburn hair. There was nothing contrary to her Oath in liking men; the only thing she had sworn herself from was becoming their property. She could even marry as a freemate if she wished, but there was about as much chance of that happening as her becoming Keeper at Arilinn. Between her Renunciate Oath and her ethics as a mid-wife—to treat the husband of the laboring woman with scrupulous integrity—she had little enough chance to find a man who might stir her heart. Which left her dreams and, at Midsummer, a single night to hope.

I've never for an instant regretted my Oath. Even if I'd stayed in my father's house and married at his bidding, nothing would have been differ-ent. She wiped her face again, a sudden tear blending with her sweat.

"Let's make camp early and hold our own Festival." Maire laughed. She stood aside for Gavi to pass, and hooked her arm through Fiona's.

"Great idea. I've got a little wine left in my bottle," said Fiona.

Gavi sighed, ignoring Maire's giggle, and kept walking along the thread of a trail. She stepped carefully over a fallen sapling, then paused, listening. Ahead lay underbrush so thick the path seemed to disappear into a wall of tangled green. Her frag-mentary *laran*, which gave her such sensitivity as a midwife, shrilled out a warning.

Maire bumped into her and stumbled, laughing, but Fiona came instantly alert. "What is it, Gavi?"

"Something ahead... But I don't hear anything."

Fiona slid her long knife soundlessly from its sheath and stepped in front of the two other women. No trace of merriment remained on her stark features. As she and Maire drew their knives, Gavi prayed she would not need to use hers. She was never a skillful fighter, and her midwife's Oath bound her to preserve and cherish life.

Like a liquid shadow, Fiona crept forward on the trail. Leafy branches parted for her as gracefully as if moved by a natural breeze. Gavi and Maire followed as quietly as they could. A moment later Gavi heard the rustle of someone moving through the brush. Here the trail ran straight and clear for a short distance.

Fiona halted and dropped into a fighting stance.

The sense of warning built like a pressure behind Gavi's heart, alarm blending into pain, pain and a cry for help. She stepped forward. "Fiona—"

Fiona jerked her head, commanding her back, just as a young man, barely out of boyhood, came hurtling along the trail. His clothing might be that of any forester, boots, leather vest over an open shirt, and loose trousers, but didn't quite fit him. He skidded to a halt, his eyes on Fiona's blade, and drew the sword at his side. Then he saw her face and threw the sword down, holding his empty hands out in a gesture of appeal.

"I mean you no harm, good women. I was headed to Rosario—for help—my master's wife—is one of you skilled in healing?"

Gavi stepped forward. "I am a midwife."

"The gods have surely smiled upon us!" The man was practically fawning on her. Only Fiona's blade, still raised and ready, kept him from throwing himself at her feet.

"Fiona, a woman needs my help—" Gavi said.

"Maire, pick up the sword. Now, lead the way, boy, and any tricks will get you your own sword in your back."

As they hurried along the trail, the man told his story in breathless snatches. He was, he said, named Felix, paxman to Valdrin, true son of old Lord Caradoc of Sweetwater in the Venza Hills—although that *nedestro* uncle had seized the manor, forcing the young lord to flee for his life.

At this point Fiona interrupted rudely, "I don't give a *cralmac's* fingernail about your local politics. You said a woman needed our help." She poked him in the back to emphasize her point.

"Yes, I understand that," Felix raised both hands and jumped forward. "His freemate—Nyssa she's called—comes from somewhere up by the Kadarin River. She's with child—never been strong—forced from her home and into the forest—"

An image rose behind Gavi's eyes: firelight gilding a woman's rounded, sweat-drenched belly, straw-colored hair tossing, eyes wide with pain. "She went into labor too soon."

"Yes, how did you know?" young Felix asked, still keeping a respectful distance from Fiona's knife.

"It's her business to know such things," said Maire grimly. "How did you think?"

They'd camped away from trailside, three sturdy chervines hidden behind the thickets. Nightfall had drenched the underbrush with shadows. As Felix hailed the camp, Gavi noticed the tent beside the fire of her vision and the clump of bodies beside it. One got up and came towards them—a man, dressed like Felix in forester's garb.

Gavi's knees turned to water. *Not even Aldones himself*, she thought, *could be so full of grace.*

In the failing daylight, his eyes were gray, but full of

brightness like a clearing storm, and his long chestnut hair fell around his princely features like a mantle. His shoulders were broad but not bulky above a dancer's hips. When he smiled and spoke, his words filled her with fire.

"May Evanda bless you, *mestra*. My wife—"

Gavi forced her eyes from the man's face and darted to the cleared area around the fire. A woman lay on piled blankets, her head cushioned on a roll of wadded garments. She wore only a thin, sweat-drenched chemise, stretched tight over her bulging abdomen. Gavi knelt beside her and took her hand.

"I'm Gavriela n'ha Alys, midwife from Thendara. How long have you been in labor?"

The woman licked her lips and grimaced, panting. Her whole body contorted suddenly, the muscles of her belly standing out. The young lord—what had Felix called him, Valdrin?—pulled her up to rest against his body, his hands cupping her shoulders protectively. Although the contraction still wracked her body, the woman's face softened as she gazed up into his face. He looked down at her with such undisguised tenderness that Gavi had to glance away.

"Since yester eve," the woman said in a low, clear voice. Her pale eyes again went to her husband's face, and her thin, six-fingered hands clutched his arm.

"But it's too soon," he said. "The baby shouldn't come for another two months."

"Yet it may live," Gavi said as positively as she could. "Or sometimes a woman is mistaken in her cycles. Let me—" Gently she laid her hand on the woman's belly to judge the size of the fetus.

Sensations flooded through her, momentarily blinding her. The first, overwhelming, was the power and alien beauty of the woman's mind. *She's* chieri, *at least half, or I'm Durraman's donkey! But she looks so womanly—perhaps because he is so manly.*

And the second was the stagnant, black presence where the life energies of the unborn child should have been.

Stunned, Gavi sat back on her heels. This was no time to indulge in sentimental maundering, not when the woman's life might be at risk. Forcing all awareness of Valdrin's magnetic beauty from her mind, she took Nyssa's hands in her own. The pale eyes met hers unflinchingly.

"You know, then?"

Nyssa nodded. "I'd hoped I was wrong."

"It's why the labor is so hard," Gavi said. "The child cannot help in its own birth."

"Nyssa," Valdrin said in a quiet, shocked voice. "You didn't tell me—"

"How could I, when you wanted this child so much? Ah—" She cried out as another contraction seized her, seized her and shook her like a rabbit-horn in the jaws of a wolf.

Gavi held her firm. "Nyssa, look at me, look at my eyes. That's right, don't see anything else. Just my eyes. Let the pain be a storm, and you a falcon sailing on its crest. Feel yourself floating on its strength, soaring. Keep breathing with me..."

The contraction ended, and Gavi shouted to Fiona and Maire to boil water and find some clean cloths. She could feel the outlines of the dead baby through Nyssa's thin abdomen. Instead of being in a normal head-down position, it lay cross-wise. There was no way it could pass the birth canal, and unless it did, Nyssa would surely die.

As calmly as she could, she explained what she had to do. "The muscles of your womb are holding the child in this bad position, so you must relax and let me turn it."

"Relax?" Valdrin asked. "When she's in such pain?"

"You must trust me, Nyssa, just as you did in that first contraction. Here, hold Valdrin's hands, and follow my voice."

Gavi talked on, using the soft murmuring tones she had learned during her years of apprenticeship. She put her hands on Nyssa's abdomen and felt the uterine muscle tense with the next contraction. The spasm raged through Nyssa's body. Gavi sank into the glowing energy fields, soothing the pain from within. She felt Nyssa, like a jeweled blossom, opening to her mental touch...

And then another mind joined theirs, like deep-hued silk, smooth and subtle, not as brilliant as Nyssa's, but blending with them both.

Eyes closed, Gavi pressed deeper into the uterine wall and felt the muscles go buttery. The dead baby, stiff and brittle, resisted her. Nyssa gave a high, breathy cry, distracting Gavi for an instant. When she returned her concentration to the stillborn, she felt another pair of hands over hers, not physical but mental, feeding her with vibrant life force. She could feel his heart beating, feel the power streaming from his loins through his body and through hers, out her fingertips and into Nyssa's womb.

As the baby slipped into the proper alignment, Gavi was deep enough to read the pattern in its dead cells, and realize that no union between this human man and this half-*chieri* woman could be viable. Her midwife trainers had mentioned *lethal recessives* as a problem of the inbred Comyn, but she never thought she'd see one.

A few minutes later, her hands half-scalded by the hot soapy water, she reached inside the laboring woman and began guiding the tiny head outward. The stillborn baby was small, even for its age. Nyssa screamed as it left her and began hemorrhaging profusely.

Gavi had no time to spare for sadness at the stillbirth. She had to act quickly, or there would be two deaths. Normally, the suckling of the infant would stop the bleeding, but now Nyssa's life blood poured forth in a heavy gush. Fearing again for the woman's life, Gavi began vigorously kneading her uterus from the outside. It took all her skill to stimulate the muscles into clamping down on the broken blood vessels without causing further injury. She scarcely noticed when Maire wrapped the baby in a bit of torn blanket and gave it to Valdrin.

It was a long, messy business getting the bleeding controlled. By the time it was done, Gavi's shirt was covered in blood and sweat, and her thighs and forearms trembled with fatigue. Pale and exhausted, Nyssa lay wrapped in cloaks from the women's packs. Gavi sat back and took a deep breath.

The camp was deserted, except for Fiona and Maire, sitting together just beyond the tent. The two men had disappeared, probably to bury the infant.

"Gavi... Gavriela."

Gavi moved to Nyssa's side and took her hand. Her fingers felt cold. "You should sleep now. Your body needs rest to repair itself."

"I won't die now?"

"I don't think so. The worst is over."

"But I mustn't conceive another child."

Gavi took a deep breath. She would have preferred to wait until Nyssa was stronger, but she couldn't lie to her now. She looked into the pale, unflinching eyes. "No. Not by Valdrin. Probably not by any man with *laran*."

"There's no other whose child I would want," she said

passionately. "And he—he loves me, but it's so important to him—to have an heir—to hold Sweetwater after him."

Gavi's thoughts flashed to her Amazon's Oath, "I will bear no child to any man may save for my own pleasure...no child for house or heritage, clan or inheritance..." But Nyssa had sworn no such Oath, and with her *chieri* sensitivity, was completely vulnerable to the depth of her husband's desires.

"I saw the way you looked at him," Nyssa continued. "And I felt—when we were together—your life energy danced with his. When we were in my body—I felt yours. I know—you are fertile now."

Gavi scuttled backwards, almost falling. Her voice came out as harsh as a *kyorebni's*. "What are you saying?"

"That you can bear his child for me."

Gavi couldn't see, couldn't think straight for the roaring in her head. Nyssa hauled herself upright with sudden, desperate vigor. She grabbed Gavi's hands in fingers of steel. "On your Amazon's Oath—no woman shall appeal to me in vain. That's what you've sworn isn't it?"

The Oath meant another Renunciate, but how could she tell Nyssa that she owed her no allegiance? As a midwife, she had sworn to nurture, to defend, to protect with all her powers, any woman in her care. If she could not bear a child for a man's choosing, what about another woman's? Would she not be saving Nyssa's life?

It would be brief and sweet, a dream to treasure for a lifetime, lying together under the moon-bright sky. Midsummer Festival night, with a god in her arms. She imagined his lips on hers, his graceful fingers curved around her breasts. Her heartbeat quickened and her nipples tingled, sending tiny tendrils of pleasure through her body.

Nyssa's fingers trembled as she held Gavi's. Her breath came fast and light, as if she were drawing on the ragged edge of her strength.

"Lie back," Gavi said gently. "You must rest now."

"Not until you say yes."

Gavi no longer knew what was right. One Oath was pitted against another, and her soaring desire clouded both. She couldn't ask Fiona or Maire for advice, either. She knew exactly what they'd say.

"Val..." Nyssa whispered. "How long have you been listening?"

Gavi twisted and looked up to see Valdrin standing a few feet behind her, shadowed by a low-hanging branch. He moved closer, the firelight burnishing his features. "Long enough," he said tightly. "Have you gone mad, Nyssa? Or do you think because I love you I am your toy to be given away to any other woman you choose, without consulting my feelings in the matter?"

Nyssa whimpered and fell back against the roll of wadded clothing. He turned as if to storm away.

"Listen!" Gavi cried, suddenly furious. "What she wanted— she wanted for *you*, you blockhead! You and that heir you want so much—she nearly died trying to give that to you, do you hear? And now you turn your back on her—"

Like a dancer, he knelt at her side. "Forgive me, my love, I didn't understand. But—"

"But if I were pregnant, or ill, and you were in need, I would send you to the woman I loved best," she murmured, reaching up to touch his face. "You've told me this is the way of your people."

He brought her hand to his lips and kissed her fingers, his

shining eyes fixed on hers. "That was—a sort of bragging."

"But true." She glanced at Gavi. "This woman can give you what I cannot. A sister's gift, with my blessing."

At first Gavi couldn't meet his eyes, not until he cupped her chin and held her. His touch was like satin, like flame. His fingers caressed her cheek, brushed her lower lip. Even in the dim firelight, his eyes held depths she'd never seen before. "And you, you are willing?"

"I don't know." She clambered to her feet, surprised at how stiff her knees were. *I'm getting older, I may never have another chance...*

A chance at what? she asked herself. *A night with another woman's man? A child already promised to her father, to live the life he makes for her? Why did I leave my father's house, if not to gain the right to choose my own life?*

He took her hand, led her towards the woods. "Let's walk a while, and talk. We need not decide in haste."

The four moons had gathered overhead, silvering the tree trunks. The forest seemed unnaturally still, a fairyland, before some bird, as if thinking it were day, erupted into song.

"I can appreciate the difficulty of your situation," he said.

"Can you? What do you know of my Oath, or my life?"

"I know you're a woman of integrity. If Nyssa—if things had been different, if you and I had met on some Midsummer Festival, and both of us free of heart, I think we might have found pleasure in one another."

Gavi's heart leapt within her. He paused, as if measuring her response. She turned away, chewing on one knuckle.

Here is an evening of pleasure, pitted against a lifetime Oath. Is it something I can set aside, simply because I wish it? Am I bound to break my Oath because a woman demands it of me in the name of sisterhood?

And if the Renunciate Oath does not give me the freedom to follow my own desires, what good is it?

Valdrin must have taken her silence for assent, for he put his hands on her shoulders and drew her closer. Her body responded to his overwhelming masculine energy, her heart beating like a captive bird, and her loins melting like butter. He bent his head and kissed her.

She almost raised her hands to put them around him. But she couldn't move, not until she knew what she truly wanted.

"Don't I please you?" he murmured, his breath gently blowing her hair.

"You do," she whispered, and then repeated it firmly, "You do. I've wanted you since the moment I saw you. But this isn't a simple Midsummer gift, it's four lives at stake. Yours, mine, Nyssa's, the child's. I have no say over what you and Nyssa do with yours."

She moved away from him and her body still quivered where he'd touched her. "But I have two Oaths that I must honor— and Oath to live my life to my own pattern, not anyone else's. And an Oath to respect my sisters, Amazon or not. What Nyssa has offered me is not something she can share. I would be wanting you to look at me the way you look at her, and that is something not she, not you, not Aldones himself, can give me."

"But—" he protested, and she cut him off, half-afraid that if he touched her again she'd forget everything that was now so clear to her.

"But I could take what you—and she—offer me, if there were not that fourth life. A life I would be twice sworn to defend. To defend not just from physical danger, but from the same enslavement I ran away from. If I bore you a child, and it was a girl, would she be free to choose her own life, even one such as mine? Or would she be pushed off on the man you thought could best hold Sweetwater?"

"No, what do you think of me?"

"And if it were a boy, would he be any more free, or would he be your heir even if his heart lead him elsewhere—to a Tower, to the cristoforos at Nevarsin?"

Valdrin hung his head, his face shadowed even in the light of the four moons. "I couldn't promise you that."

"I know," she said gently. "And if you were not a man such as you are, I would not be so tempted." She kissed him gently, a sister's kiss.

"Your wife is waiting for you. Go back, and pray Aldones to make you worthy of her."

After he'd left, she stood among the trees, wondering how she'd remember this night, and what it might have been. *Talk about sentimental maundering!*

Shadows moved beneath the trees. Fiona and Maire, their knives drawn, stepped into the moonlight. "I see you didn't need any help after all," Fiona said.

Gavi raised her eyebrows. "Fiona, have you still got that wine? Let's get it out and celebrate Midsummer together."

Fiona gave a whoop of delight as they headed back toward the camp, their arms around each other.

Wasteland

They came by night, in silent ambush. Rorie Leynier held himself very still, ready for them, still clothed and curled in a parody of sleep beside the embers of his campfire. His starstone lay mute on his breast, yet he knew they were out there, hunting him, waiting for the moment to attack.

Without warning, a huge bulk of a man loomed over him, blade edge glimmering in Kyrrdis's blue light. Rorie lashed out with one booted foot as he reached for his sword and rolled away from the banked fire. The attacker fell forward with a muffled cry that turned into a shriek of pain as sparks flew beneath him and his beard burst into flame.

Even as he twisted, Rorie's nostrils filled with the stench of seared human flesh. The big man who had fallen rolled free, beating out the small fires in his hair with oaths so coarse as to be unintelligible. Rorie recognized enough of the dialect to realize that his assailants were no more than outlaws come ravening down from the heights in search of easier prey.

Rorie's horse, tethered beyond the perimeter of the camp, whickered and stamped her feet. His muscles tightened as he gauged the distance to her.

Too far, he thought, and his back bare to the jackals the

whole way. He felt the others close in—if only he could see where they were!

Hands reached for him from the darkness, hands that only seemed human but tore like Zandru's demons at his throat and sides. Rorie wrenched away from them, slashing with his sword. He felt the blade tip catch, then rip through fabric. A quick, shuffling step brought him closer, and this time, there was an answering cry to his thrust. He'd wounded one of them, but just how badly he could not tell.

Without consciously willing it, he jerked aside before a knife came humming out of the night, angled low to hamstring him. His sword slid along the shorter blade, barely stopping at the guard to slice through fingers and beyond to softer flesh.

Gods! How could they see him, when all his eyes brought him were shadows of blue and dimmest red?

Then he remembered what Mirelle, his Keeper at Corandolis Tower had told him when she'd sent him away as unfit for even the meanest work—that whatever flawed his *laran* talents also impaired his night vision. It was not that the dark was so dense, but that he himself could not penetrate its blackness.

Blind, blind! Now he was fighting for his skin, dodging the short, deadly blades more by intuition than knowledge.

Worthless to Tower and family he might be, Rorie thought angrily, but he was still Comyn and deserved a better fate than to fall to trail scum like this. Without conscious thought he turned, slicing in a downward arc, and heard a cry that marked the end of another attacker.

The slain outlaw fell slowly, as if death had given his flesh a curious lightness, and landed in the remains of the fire. Sparks leapt momentarily in puffs of singed hair that quickly died into stillness.

Rorie gathered his feet under him and tightened his grip on his sword. Without the fire's glow, the dim light of one small moon was not enough to give a significant visual advantage over his attackers. Now they were equally blind, and foolish enough to give away their positions by shouting at each other.

With adrenaline pounding through his veins, Rorie forced himself to move softly, angling away from the nearest outlaw and towards his mare. Now that he was no longer straining for vision, he could hear all four remaining assailants, the big chief slashing about with his blade. One man, to Rorie's left, stood still and began fumbling with something—a flint to relight the fire?

He had no choice now, no luxury to inch cautiously towards his horse. Rorie sprinted across the remaining distance, praying that he would be able to scramble on the mare's back before the outlaws dragged him from her.

The horse pranced as Rorie cut her tether line and grabbed a handful of mane. Aldones be praised, she was sweet-tempered enough to stand while he threw his right leg over her back.

She leaped forward as the first of the outlaws reached her, hands stretching toward the dangling end of her halter rope. Rorie slashed down at him, and the mare shuddered as her rider's desperation seized her, then wheeling and lashing out with her front hooves.

Now they were in the open, running with a shared need for escape. Rorie clung to his sword with one hand, the other entangled in the mare's wind-whipped mane. The muscles of her back flexed and knotted beneath his thighs. Once she stumbled, going down almost to her knees, and the sharp bones of her withers dug into his crotch as he lurched forward.

Rorie could hear shouts from behind. They were following,

so they must have had mounts of their own hidden nearby. Then the mare was on her feet again, once more a creature ruled by panic. Between the disjointed scramble of her gallop and the rampaging of his own heart, Rorie could hear nothing more.

He lost all sense of time and direction, barely noticing the changing terrain and shifting multihued shadows. Idriel and pearly Mormallor rose to join Kyrrdis, and he became aware that he had left his pursuers far behind. Perhaps they had returned to the camp, content with its booty.

Rorie made no attempt to guide the mare with his knees or reach forward to grab the trailing stub of rope swinging from her halter. The passing terrain was a swirl of murky shadows, and her night vision must serve for both of them. Eventually the mare slowed, her sides heaving like great bellows. The thin leather of Rorie's breeches was soaked with their mingled sweat, which had turned acrid with fear. Heat rose from their bodies like a cloud of steam in the cool night.

Rorie shifted his weight and the mare came to a weary halt, head lowered. He looked down at the sword clenched in his hand, its blade glimmering faintly in the light of three moons, and realized he was trembling. He slid to the ground, looped his belt into a makeshift sling for the sword, and began to walk his horse to cool her down. He told himself that his present situation might be bleak, but it would be bleaker still if he lost her due to carelessness.

He remembered thinking, as he had made camp only a few short hours ago, that his life could not be much more dismal, being the extraneous fourth son of a family richer in heirs than lands, now being sent home as useless by the Tower that had once seemed like his only chance to find a place for himself. Rorie snorted at his pathetic self-pity, and reached over to scratch the mare's sweaty ears.

Now look at the mess he'd gotten himself into! Like the game that walked from the trap to the cook pot, he'd lost his food, saddle, extra clothing, in short, everything but what he'd slept in, one sword without a proper sheath, and a loyal but tired mount. On the other hand, he still had his life, and he wondered if even a normally-sighted man could have done as well against the trail scum that had jumped him, grown bold by the disorder that still lingered after the signing of the Compact.

The night hung quiet and heavy around him, silent except for the susurration of breathing and the occasional clink of halter ring or creak of the makeshift sword sheath. Even their footsteps seemed hushed, unnatural. Eventually the mare cooled and Rorie wrapped the halter rope around one hand and sat down, making himself as comfortable as he could. His head fell forward on arms crossed around his knees and finally he slept.

Rorie awoke to pain, a pulsating ache over his sternum. He sat upright, blinking in the gray morning light. He put one hand to his chest, half-expecting to find his shirt slick with congealed blood, but felt nothing except his starstone. Even though he had wrapped it in insulating silk as he had been taught at the Tower, it throbbed insistently. He forced his eyes into focus.

The mare stood beside his feet, nuzzling his boots as if considering their suitability as fodder. The severed rope had slipped from his fingers and lay trailing in the dust. Dust...

Rorie froze as his eyes took in his surroundings. Dust, gray and lifeless, covered the ground, the few withered skeletons of bush and tree, and the low hills rising before him. He could not spy a single blade of grass or buzzing insect. Except for the thunder of his own heart and the mare's soft breathing, they were two alone in a desolation of monochromatic dust.

Bonewater dust.

He had thought himself safe in the hills, far enough from the lands blasted sterile by the terrible *laran* weapons of the Age of Chaos. The wasteland had been marked on his maps, but sketchily, as if the cartographer had not wanted to dwell on its exact parameters. Somehow, in the terror of the night attack, in his blindness and the mare's panic, they had wandered so far into the wasteland that it now surrounded them.

Surrounded them, the insidious particles already working their way through his body's defenses. Rorie gasped, then fought his breathing under control. Was he even now drawing the deadly stuff into his lungs where it would invade his entire body, turning his bones to crumbling ash? Would his flesh melt into jelly as his blood thinned to rosewater while his brain, functional to the last, watched helplessly?

He shivered, drawing upon his hard-won skills to monitor himself for the first signs of internal rot. Even though he unwrapped his starstone and gripped it, he sensed no deviation from the normal workings of his body. Nothing was amiss, not in himself nor in the mare.

Of course, he thought bitterly, *what did he expect?* The few poor techniques they had managed to drill into him at Corandolis were just that: useless yearnings. Not enough to save him, now when he most needed them.

He got to his feet, brushing the grit from his pants. The mare, undisturbed, pricked her ears at him in mild curiosity. Slinging the sword through his leather belt, he swung on to her back, hoping against hope that from that vantage point he would be able to tell the direction from which they had come and might now return.

It was no use. Gray dust, gray hills, and gray, twisted remains of plant life stretched as far as his eyes could see in all directions. Nor did the shifting layers of powder-fine dust hold any trace of hoof prints from the night before. The red sun lay directionless behind veils of clouds, and the air was chill and sullen, and unnaturally still.

Rorie grasped the end of the halter rope but made no attempt to guide the mare as he nudged her forward. Her instincts might not warn her of the insidious dangers of the place, but surely, given her head, she would seek out water and grazing, and a way out of this nightmarish place. Maybe there was still some slim hope, he thought. But he did not believe it.

Time seemed suspended as man and horse traveled on through the bleak, silent landscape. Rorie found his mind numbed and unresponsive, as if some essential part of him had already surrendered to the poisoned land. Even the mare's lack of concern struck him as hopeless, a token of her dumb beast nature rather than her keen survival instincts. The motion of her gait loosened the fear-tightened muscles of his back and thighs, gradually coaxing him into a hypnotic rhythm. He surrendered to it as he did to his own overwhelming despair.

Rorie was so caught up in the mesmeric certainty of his own doom that he nearly toppled forward over the mare's neck when she came to an abrupt halt. He grabbed her mane with his free hand and righted himself. They had come to the top of a rise and stood looking down over a narrow, river-etched valley.

At the exact center, cupped by the surrounding hills, stood a Tower.

And such a Tower as Rorie had never in his short life seen,

or even dreamt. Even in the diffuse red light, it gleamed, opalescent and luminous as if its foundations were mixed with starstone chips. Its soaring lines spoke of grace and confidence, of building techniques far beyond mere human masonry. And it stood intact in its glory, untouched by the desolation that surrounded it. Corandolis, or even the great Tower at Hali seemed but a poor imitation of its grandeur. Indeed, he thought as he felt a tremor run through the mare's body, such a Tower had not existed in the Domains for many a long year, not since the height of Comyn madness.

Rorie let out his breath and the mare started forward at a brisk trot, her ears pricked forward. Without any urging, she broke into a jolting canter, sweeping down the hill towards the gleaming Tower.

The gates stood before them, open and majestic. As Rorie drew near, a slender figure clad in shimmering blue darted forward, hands outstretched in welcome, long red hair like a banner behind her.

A girl. A Comyn girl.

Rorie hauled on the mare's halter rope, drawing her to a clattering halt just inside the Tower gates. His eyes fastened on the girl, seeing that she was no child but a young and beautiful woman. Beyond her a fountain played in a courtyard, and he caught a flash of living green that marked a garden strip.

"Blessed Cassilda, you've come!" she cried, reaching up to steady the mare's head. She looked up at him with wide green eyes set in a perfect heart-shaped face, her cheeks delicately flushed with rose. She met his gaze with a directness that could only come from years of Tower training, and he caught the unmistakable tang of powerful *laran*.

"I—I don't understand," Rorie managed to stammer. His

heart raced as much with her disturbingly feminine presence as with the discovery of the Tower. "What are you doing here?"

She shook her head, her hair rippling with light like a glorious copper mane. "I was so worried while I was alone, but everything's going to be all right now that you're here to help. Please, get down. Can I get you anything? Water? Food? Fodder for your horse?"

Rorie responded to the subtle hint of command in her voice and slid from the mare's back. "Water, I think. To wash the dust away." His unspoken thought: *Would that do any good now?*

She laughed, leading the way towards the fountain. "I too feared so at first, but even handicapped as it is, this circle has great healing powers. Here I am as proof, alive and whole."

The mare plunged her nose into the clear water without hesitation as Rorie rinsed his face and hands. Again he turned to the Comyn lady. "Who are you? What are you doing here, in the middle of this...?"

"I'm Shani, originally trained at—but that was a long time ago. I won't ask what Tower you're from. What matters, Rorie, is what we can do together now. We are both needed so desperately."

Rorie looked away from the intensity of her eyes, realizing that her skill was such that she could pick up his name and his reticence to recount his expulsion from the Tower. "What do you need me for?"

"You know what this place is?"

"A Tower, intact but apparently abandoned, surrounded by a bonewater dust wasteland."

"Bonewater dust, aye." Shani nodded. "Only one of the many terrible *laran* weapons used by one Domain against another. But although this Tower, whose very name has been lost, was attacked, it was not destroyed."

"Yes, I can see that."

"The Tower circle is still intact, along with bits of its matrix screens."

"That can't be possible, not after hundreds of years."

"I'll show you in a moment. But think—how else could these turrets still stand? How else could there be a fountain of pure water, and safe food for human and beast?"

Rorie could find no answer, but followed Shani through a graceful arched doorway and into the central tower. They crossed the common room with its comfortable furniture and generous fireplace, everything looking as fresh and undisturbed as if it were currently inhabited. Rorie would have thought the Tower still in daily use, but there was an unnatural density in the shadows that told him it had been a long time since anyone sat on those pillows or lit a blaze on that cold hearth.

The stairway was broad, as open and airy as the rest of the Tower. Built using *laran* forces, without the constraints of human limitations, it clearly indulged the Darkovan love of sweeping spaces and natural lighting.

Rorie felt the energies of the central Tower room even before they entered. It was like nearing a vast, immense battery in which barely checked forces surged and flowed. Even with his meager talents, even with his starstone shrouded in insulating silk, the power of the place clawed hungrily at him. The hairs on the back of his neck rose.

Shani turned back to him with sympathy in her green eyes. "It's all right, really. Just a little alarming at first because of the magnitude of the matrix, but it's perfectly safe. The circle has it well under control." She swung aside the door and stepped back for him to enter.

Rorie stepped into a wide, circular room, furnished in comfort to the point of luxury. On a round table sat the huge crystal, alive with blue and silver...and nine men and women, robed in opulence and bathed in flickering light. Their features bore the unmistakable stamp of their superb *laran*, refined through generations of breeding and rigorous training. They were all young and beautiful, their hair in shades of flaming, almost arrogant red, rising and falling in gentle waves as they gazed intently at the central gem.

"The circle," Shani whispered. "Just as they looked when they locked themselves out of time in that final, fatal battle. No one knows who they fought, or why. All we can see is the wasteland that is the result...and this little island of safety they managed to carve out for themselves."

"I don't see that it's done them much good," Rorie said. "Even if they freed themselves, how could they escape the bonewater disease? Surely if they had that power, they would have done so long ago, without any small measure of help I might be able to lend them." *And*, he thought, *how do I know they were the ones defending themselves and not the perpetrators of the desolation outside? Even if it were possible, could I dare risk turning loose telepaths of that magnitude with no loyalty to the Compact?*

He thought of Mirelle, Keeper of Corandolis, and her perpetual caution, her insistence that *laran* be used only for safe, Compact-legal purposes, and also of her underlying fear that would not let her acknowledge any talent she could not control.

"Weren't you listening?" The musical tones of Shani's voice, even in scolding, shook him from his doubts. "They used the matrix screen to shield themselves and, to a lesser extent, the whole Tower. There's been no energy left over for any voluntary action. Here they've sat, locked into their own salvation. But with my *laran*—and yours—we can give them the edge they need to break free. Then they can use the starstone to cleanse the land so it can live again. Isn't that worth taking a small risk for?"

"I don't know. Even if I could...even if I could—"

"Do you doubt my judgment?" Shani's question whipped out with the unmistakable authority of a Keeper. The starstone between her breasts blazed. "Or are you the proverbial blind man denying the existence of color just because it is beyond his own senses?"

Rorie shrugged. Just as he had not argued with Mirelle when he'd been dismissed from Corandolis Tower, so now he felt he had no basis for denying Shani's claim. Her own trained talent was evident in her every gesture, and he was acutely aware of his own limitations.

She nodded, smiling slightly. Was there just the hint of satisfaction in that smile?

Are you going to doubt everything? Rorie demanded of himself. *What a pitiful means of salving the remnants of your self-esteem.*

Shani gestured to him, brushing her fingertips so close to his wrist that he felt a slight shock of energy, although no actual contact. He recognized it as a classical Keeper's touch: evanescent, suggestive, noncommittal.

"There is your place," she said in a low, throaty voice, "there..." She nodded towards a break in the spacing of the entranced circle workers. "And there is mine."

Rorie thought for a moment that the seat she indicated as hers must be the Keeper's place, but he immediately dismissed the idea as ridiculous. Shani, for all her obvious training, was no part of the original circle, but a wanderer like himself, attracted by the concentration of *laran* power, and then held by the

Tower's demanding need and her own compassion.

"We join the circle, then?" he asked.

Shani stood behind him as if to help him take his seat. Rorie turned his head to see her eyes upon him like luminous green gems, like a falcon scanning the burrows of a rabbit-horn. His palms felt suddenly chill and moist. Clumsily he began to lower himself on to the padded bench, lost his balance momentarily, and reached out a hand to steady himself.

As his fingers passed through the outer edge of the energon rings, tremendous forces sparked along Rorie's nerves. He gasped. He had known the matrix to be powerful, but had had no conception of its true magnitude. No wonder it was capable of focusing enough *laran* to preserve the Tower workers through the years, even against bonewater dust and equally terrible weapons. Even its outer edge, casually touched, was strong enough to stop a man's heart.

He blinked, his vision darkening...and froze. For superimposed upon the images of the men and women of the circle, frozen in timeless concentration and beauty, were the lineaments of horror. Those serene faces were but tissue coverings for decay, shreds of charred flesh hanging in strips from whitened bone. Sickly blue light played over the eye sockets, faintly reflected within. Instead of gracefully cupped hands, he saw skeletal claws, suspended in agony around a pulsating maw of raw psychic hunger.

Through the borders of his awareness howled the traces of their death agonies—not, as Rorie had first suspected, in sadness and defeat, grasping at a last, desperate hope for survival—but betrayal, the searing pain of souls forever condemned to a hell of their own making.

The circle had not, as Shani had said, preserved themselves

91

through the giant matrix stone. It had been an instrument of desolation for so long, focused on unthinkable evil, that in the end it had acquired a consciousness of its own, with only one goal—to survive. They had reached for its power in their last frenzied moments, only to be devoured, drained of their precious *laran* energies until only husks remained. Once they had been powerful telepaths, the best of a whole tradition of selective inbreeding and exhaustive training, these men and women of the unknown Tower. Their energies had fed the stone for many a long year.

Now its reserves had dwindled, its energy waned, and even the wasteland in which it lay like a perverted jewel gave it no sustenance. It had reached out and drawn Rorie into its web, as it had caught Shani before him.

He had to warn her, get her out of there, get both of them out of there, before it was too late. The appearance of the circle was but an illusion, their need nothing but a thin veil for the ravening hunger of the stone.

"Sh—hani! I think—" He stumbled, fumbling for the words to warn her, yet not alert whatever parody of intelligence might lurk within the stone. "I need to rest a bit before we try. I'm—you know my *laran* isn't very strong, and I've had a hard night."

Rorie stood up, carefully avoiding any further contact with the energon fields of the giant matrix, and turned to her.

He saw her beauty, and the subtle blend of feminine seductiveness and Keeper isolation she spun about herself. But underneath, pervading the whole image, lay corruption as rank and vile as he had seen in the circle. Rorie knew then that Shani was indeed the Keeper of the circle, and it had been through her that the others had been sucked dry. Twisted blue light flickered behind her eyes, and for a fleeting moment he caught the odor of a charnel house on her sweet breath. The mark of the giant starstone lay upon her like a veil of death. She opened her rosebud mouth, and he saw the rotten skull gape its jaws in anticipation.

Rorie grabbed her by the shoulders, dimly aware that he was committing the most unthinkable assault upon the person of a Tower-trained woman, a Keeper who should have been immune from even a thought of an unwanted touch. Desperately he pulled her over the bench, using his hips and thigh muscles to swivel around and thrust her into the very center of the matrix.

She screamed, a piercing wail. Tentacles of coruscating blue fire leapt from the heart of the crystal, lashing towards Rorie's heart. He threw himself backwards, but the padded bench caught him at the back of his knees, slowing his fall. The nerves of his skin shrieked as the energon fields seized him.

As the matrix dragged him within its surging core, Rorie could no longer feel his mortal body. He could only imagine the convulsions that shook his frame again and again. Now he was at the heart of the stone, riddled by its lightnings. He experienced energy as a visual sensation, vivid as his usual vision never was, as it tossed him in its tumultuous sphere. He could sense shadows of the minds that had gone before him, thin echoes of once-vibrant personalities, now worn into crusts by time and the relentless drain of the matrix.

The center of the thing loomed before him, a maw of blackness, of not-being, pulsating and puckering as if already welcoming him into itself. Every fiber of Rorie's consciousness shrank from it, for it boded not simple oblivion but a mental slavery that would endure century after century until the last wisp of awareness departed from his spirit.

As he struggled against the pull of the matrix, Rorie

wondered what use it could have for him. He could understand the crystal's lust for a powerful, trained talent such as those who had comprised the original circle...or any of the Tower workers he had studied with. But he had been sent from Corandolis Tower as inadequate, unfit. Mirelle, his Keeper, had said so in no uncertain terms. How could he have within him enough *laran* to be of any value to the matrix?

Then he realized the matrix was not a living, thinking being, but a mockery of one, and as such it was not subject to the delusions and preconceptions of a human mind. It didn't know he was no good; no Keeper had, for personal or political reasons, ever told it so. Therefore it had relied only on its own limited perception of him—and that perception had told it that within Rorie lay the force it needed to continue its parasitic existence. There must be something inside him, something his own Keeper had been blind to, the way he was blind in the darkness. Perhaps, the thought seeped through his draining consciousness, perhaps she had sensed it in him, but shrank from it in a reflex conditioned by fear and guilt.

Perhaps the same ability that limited his night sight—Rorie could no longer consider it a flaw—also gave him the true vision of the circle corpses—also let him see the matrix for the evil thing it was—and would also give him what he needed to conquer it.

Anger flared up in him, hot and red in contrast to the livid blue of the matrix. He fed it with his will to live, the same determination that had refused to give up when the bandits attacked him the night before. *How dare this thing, this mere inanimate mass of crystal and energy ring dare to destroy a human mind, feeding on precious Comyn talents without conscience or reason—could there be any greater sin, and more obscene insult to the gods?*

Machine! roared through Rorie's thoughts. *It's nothing but a Compact-banned machine!* If he had been in his physical body he would have spat on it in outrage. But righteous indignation alone could not conquer the vastly powerful starstone that held him in its inexorable grip, slowly closing in to drag him into its core.

His physical body... He could feel it, half-crouched against the padded bench.

Hand—he must move his hand! He thrust his will into the command and felt the shadow-hand move towards the hilt of his sword. The white and blue energies of the crystal crackled around him, protesting even this small freedom.

Rorie hardened his determination. Whatever it was the stone resisted, that thing he would do with all his might.

Lungs—inhale! Heart—beat! Shoulder muscles—tighten! Hand to sword hilt! Could he actually feel its texture beneath his shadow fingers, or was it merely an illusion born of his fevered desire?

Yes, he could see the sword sliding through its makeshift sheath, the glimmer of steel before his shadow eyes. Caustic blue light played reflections across the blade's polished surface.

Other hand—grasp...wrists—flex—

In frenzy, the matrix tightened its stranglehold on him, smothering him with its power as it drew him in. Rorie realized that with every effort to control his physical body, he weakened his mental defenses against it. He knew he could not defeat the matrix on its own terms. His only chance for survival lay in his unique ability to stay outside of its chosen sphere of battle, to see the illusions it created as they really were—and now to use the physical dimension to his own advantage.

Rorie relinquished his psychic resistance to the crystal, throwing his strength and will into his real body. The muscles of his hands tightened around the leather-wrapped sword hilt. His abdomen hardened as he brought his weight to bear, slashing down, as he aimed the tempered blade at the center of the starstone.

Splinters flew in every direction, shattering the light at the heart of the demented crystal. For an eternal fraction of a moment, Rorie-within-the-starstone and Rorie-without were blinded, buffeted, ground to quivering fragments under the explosive assault. His ears brought him the frantic, keening death-wail of the thing, his pupils constricted in denial of the poisonous white nova before him.

Gradually sensation returned to him: tears dripping from his face, the heat in his hands as they touched his blackened sword, and the trembling of his thigh muscles. He dropped the molten blade and sat back on the bench, aware of its unsteadiness but unable to support his own weight any longer.

Rorie's vision cleared with agonizing slowness as he made out details before him. The table that had supported the matrix crystal sagged crazily, tilting under its burden of lightless shards. Bones disjointed and crumbled into piles of grayish ash. From somewhere outside came the frantic whinny of a horse.

The mare. Rorie gathered his legs under him as the bench collapsed completely. As he turned towards the stairwell, he saw cracks widening through the dull stone of the turret. Once the sustaining power of the matrix was withdrawn, time and decay would have their way at last.

But the courtyard was not a desolate ruin. Water still bubbled from the tumbled stone of the fountain, and healthy green sprouted everywhere. Rorie grabbed the mare's halter rope and patted her sweating neck. She rolled her eyes and danced nervously at the falling chunks of stone, and followed him through the sagging gates.

Rorie had expected to see gray bonewater dust stretching to the horizon, but even the wasteland had been transformed by the destruction of the starstone. Devastation had wracked this land, certainly, but it had been far in the past, and now Evanda's bounty touched it once again, bringing little clumps of green.

Rorie halted the mare to look back at the Tower, still collapsing in on itself. He did not know why the crystal had maintained the illusion of death and devastation—perhaps as an additional defense against the re-establishment of Comyn rule? What merely human mind could comprehend its motivation?

The mare pulled at the halter and bent her head for a mouthful of tender grass. Rorie let her graze as he unwrapped his own starstone.

Instead of its usual dim blue light, the gem blazed with a complex dance of reflected brilliance. Rorie realized that his confrontation with the matrix had activated his unusual latent talents, talents his own Keeper had been unwilling to recognize.

Willingly had the Towers participated in the warfare of the Age of Chaos. Willingly they might have worked to halt the destruction, but the time was not yet when they might pretend it had never happened. It was still and everlastingly their responsibility to erase all traces of that evil from the face of Darkover.

And how do you know this? Rorie challenged himself. His *laran* might be, indeed, flawed or unusable, but he himself was Comyn, however minor his house. His caste had signed the Compact with their own blood. And if some fear-blinded Keeper would not face up to her responsibility, by Aldones he would compel her.

But the Towers were not all weak and self-serving, and the

telepaths who worked in them had a right to know of the thing that had laid its deadly trap in the wasteland.

Rorie focused on the glittering depths of his starstone, reaching out with an ease he had never known before.

Corandolis, he called.

The response came from the kindly, middle-aged technician working the relay screens: *Rorie? Is that young Rorie?*

Rorie could feel the strength of his *laran* blasting along the pathways, ringing with urgency and command: *I have found something that concerns the honor of us all. Mirelle must come.*

Wait...

And then the Keeper's mind touched his: *We will come in answer to a Comyn equal who calls us as is his right. I will know where to find you...* Mirelle's telepathy bore no trace of surprise or dismay. As always, her emotions lay buried under unbreakable control, and Rorie know he would never receive a hint of apology for the injustice done to him.

Rorie wrapped his starstone in insulating silk as Mirelle's mental touch faded from his mind. He did not know if his recent growth and trials would change her mind about his place in the Tower. He did not know if he even wanted it, but he was finished thinking of himself as something flawed, inadequate, and for the moment that was enough.

Cradle of Lies

As the funeral procession wound through Hali, Ashara Alton thought there was no more fitting tribute to Varzil the Good than the mysterious, cloud-filled lake that he had restored. The Keepers of half the Towers on Darkover had come to honor Varzil and now, to the solemn, measured rhythm of the dirge, they bore his silk-shrouded body to the ancient *rhu fead* where his bones would rest, along with the other holy things, until the end of time. A few wept openly, and others masked their grief behind stony expressions. Many of the great lords had set aside their feuding for these days of mourning. Varzil had touched them all with his wisdom, healing the wounds of war and chaos, even the devastating effects of the Cataclysm that had devastated the lake.

I had not thought to follow him so soon. Ashara pulled her mourning robes closer as she walked in her proper place as under-Keeper of Neskaya Tower. To most people she seemed a slip of a girl, barely taller than a child, with delicate features and eyes so pale they seemed almost colorless. But Varzil had seen through her frail appearance.

"Your body may be small, but your spirit is pure blue fire," he'd told her when she first came to Neskaya Tower.

Remembering, Ashara stumbled on the matrix-smoothed pavement. Her heart brimmed with pain, a heaviness too great to bear. The moment of weakness passed in a heartbeat. Ashara drew upon the training Varzil had given her, her and her alone, to fulfill her promise, he'd said. To become the first woman Keeper of Neskaya.

"They'll fight you, the other Keepers," he'd warned her. "You must prepare yourself constantly, without mercy, to be even stronger than they are."

I am your successor, Varzil, and nothing they can do will take that away from me.

The evening after Varzil's funeral, every Tower worker present, from the oldest Keeper to the youngest novice, gathered in the central hall of Hali Tower. Ashara, seated with the others from Neskaya, kept her eyes downcast, but her nerves tingled with the assembled *laran* power. Deep within her, something ached to reach out, grasp that power, and bend it to her will. It was, Varzil said, the same instinct that would someday make her a Keeper, one of the most powerful the Domains had ever known.

Arnad Delleray, Keeper of Arilinn, rose to his feet. Torchlight glinted off his silvery hair. The oldest living Keeper, he had been most bitterly opposed to Varzil's plan to train women as Keepers. As he addressed the convocation, he betrayed no hint of any grief. All the tributes had been spoken, all the rites performed. He reminded them of the historical uniqueness of what they were to do. Traditionally, each Keeper chose his own successor, tested him, trained him.

As Varzil trained me, Ashara thought.

"Now it lies before us, acting as the united voice of the Towers, to choose a new Keeper for Neskaya," Arnad said.

Ellimara Aillard of Corandolis Tower rose to her feet and the room rustled as people turned to look at her. She was not only Keeper, but Comynara in her own right, and no one dared challenge her privilege to speak. "It is known that Varzil chose and trained but a single under-Keeper. Surely he intended her to take his place. It would be presumptuous for any of us to question that judgment."

A murmur rippled across the room. Ashara's *laran*-aided senses caught hushed comments. "She can't be serious.""What did you expect? She's a woman, too.""The only woman Keeper—and likely to remain so, if you ask me!"

Arnad swept the assembly with a stern glance and they quieted immediately. "Who wishes to speak on this question?"

"I do." Mikhail Storn-Aillard, Keeper of Comyn Tower, got to his feet. He wore his dark red hair long, curling over his shoulders and blending with his black beard like a living mantle. "Varzil was an innovator, always questioning and trying new things. Who else could have reversed the effects of the Cataclysm and restored the lake? Who else could have brought the great lords together to talk of peace? Yet even Varzil realized that not all experiments succeed and new ideas take time to be accepted. I believe that training women as Keepers is one of them. Our cousin Ellimara—" referring to their distant kinship, "—is proof that women can serve in this way. But just because one woman is talented enough does not mean that all women are qualified. More than that, we are not here to debate the role of *all* women." He took a deep breath, puffing up the considerable bulk of his chest. "We are here to discuss who would best serve Neskaya as Keeper."

The response was so loud, Arnad had to lift his voice to call for order. Around the room, several people had risen to their feet, waiting to be acknowledged to speak. Ashara was one of them. She held herself proudly, chin raised. Arnad's eyes rested on hers for a long moment. Then he turned away and nodded to one of the Arilinn monitors.

Ashara's hands curled into fists as she sat down. Clearly, she was not going to be allowed to speak. Or believed, no matter what she said. With a growing sense of futility, she listened as the discussion proceeded to possible candidates. Some of them, she realized, had less training than she. None of them had worked directly with Varzil.

Ashara glanced at the other workers from Neskaya and shuddered. How could she have been so blind, not to see it before, the fear of change, the smoldering resentment that she, Varzil's favorite, had advanced when they had not?

She forced her thoughts back to the debate. Tramontana Tower had several under-Keepers, including a man past the usual age of advancement. Corus MacAran was from a good family and Mikhail of Comyn Tower vouched for his competence.

Ashara turned cold. She'd met Corus once or twice and found him to be ambitious and more interested in getting her to bed with him at Midsummer Festival than in the quality of her *laran*. And he was not even here—no one from either Tramontana or Dalereuth had been able to make the long journey in time.

They would prefer a man they have not seen and cannot question to a woman who stands before them, ready to pass any test they set for her!

Ashara could not longer hold herself still. She rose to her

102

feet again, trembling with the effort needed to maintain control. She did not know it, but her powerful *laran* made her glow slightly, like an activated matrix. The room fell silent and everyone looked in her direction.

"I cannot allow this," she said in her clear, light voice. "Not without speaking the truth." Once she'd begun talking, the words seemed to flow from her. Her trembling eased.

"Varzil is not here to tell you what he wished. Believe what you will, he intended for me to be Keeper at Neskaya after him. But if it is not to be, I must accept the will of this council and serve in any way I can." She paused, her pale eyes flickering from face to face. "But not under Corus MacAran. He may be proficient enough as an under-Keeper, but he knows nothing of what Varzil was trying to accomplish at Neskaya—and if he had any gift as a Keeper, he would have been one in his own Tower long before this."

Mikhail jumped to his feet, his voice thundering through the hall. "Is there any question now that this girl is unfit to be a Keeper?"

Within a few moments, Corus MacAran was confirmed as Neskaya's new Keeper. Word would be sent to him over the matrix relays to depart at once.

Raimond Lindir, Keeper of Hali, rose to speak. A tall, thin man, he was so fair it was easy to believe that *chieri* blood ran strong in his family. Ashara knew him only from the relays and had admired his detachment and proficiency. "We cannot afford to discard a *laran* talent like Ashara's. With proper training she might become a great asset. If there is some difficulty of her continuing at Neskaya under Corus MacAran, she may remain here with us at Hali."

"We have no other under-Keeper," said one of the Neskaya

technicians. "To lose Ashara now would leave us greatly understaffed."

"Then you will return to Neskaya to serve under your new Keeper," Arnad of Arilinn told Ashara sternly. "And we will hear no more prattle about your childish whims or secret ambitions, do you understand?"

Ashara bowed her head in apparent submission. Anything she said now would cost her not only Neskaya, her home, but a place in any Tower.

Varzil, I will not betray your dream! I will find a way, I swear it!

Once he had established himself at Neskaya Tower, Corus MacAran summoned Ashara to the laboratory that he had taken over for his private work. She expected a difficult interview, but to her surprise, he was courteous, almost affable. "You're one of our strongest matrix workers and I need you for my special project."

Ashara said carefully, "I'm scheduled to supervise the newer technicians on the relays."

"Forget that, it's just routine. I'll assign someone else to do it. I want you to take charge of this section." He indicated a table heaped with papers.

Her curiosity aroused, Ashara bent over the top diagram. She understood the antiquarian notations well enough, but she'd never seen anything them before. They seemed to describe part of some larger device.

"What is it?" she asked.

"Oh, you'll see when it all comes together," Corus said. The edge in his voice told her that if she asked too many questions, she'd quickly find herself removed from the project.

Varzil would not have treated me like a child, she thought, bowing her head. *And the day will come when you will not, either.*

Ashara sat alone in the darkness, to all appearances as cold and unmoving as the bare stone of the walls of her narrow room. Around her, the Tower's living quarters lay silent, sleeping. Only Ashara kept her self-imposed vigil, drilling herself in the focusing techniques Varzil had taught her.

At first, Ashara did not stir at the sound of knocking at her door. She blinked, settled her awareness properly in her body, unfolded her legs, and went to the door. Bellisma, the young novice who worked with her on Corus's project, stood there, trembling so violently that the candle in her hand spattered drops of wax on the stone floor.

Ashara's heightened perception quickly took in the swollen energy channels in the younger woman's body. "Blessed Cassilda protect us, what has happened to you?"

"I—" Bellisma slumped suddenly.

Ashara caught her and dragged her to the bed. The candle fell and guttered out, but Ashara needed no light. She bent over the barely-conscious girl, skimming her hands over Bellisma's torso. The congested channels pulsated, glowing dull, dark red. Bellisma's heart fluttered like a caged bird's.

Ashara clamped her lips together. She knew what had happened. Bellisma was a pretty girl, physically mature for her age. Ashara had seen the way Corus looked at her, had heard him speak about what a waste it was to remain celibate while not working the great energon rings. "This nonsense about 'keeping virgin for the Sight' is nothing but superstition," he'd said.

And now the girl's awakening sexuality completely obstructed the very same channels that should be carrying her *laran*. Powerful energies, deprived of their natural flow, threatened to overload vital organ systems. She was only ill now, but if she tried to work in this condition, she might very well die

Silently Ashara gave thanks that her childish appearance had deterred most advances; she'd been fortunate that her cycles had not yet begun and perhaps never would, thanks to the strenuousness of her training.

Clearing the girl's blocked channels was simple enough, any properly trained monitor could do it. But that would not end the problem, Ashara knew. The austere discipline Varzil had demanded of the Tower was slipping away. No wonder Bellisma had come to Ashara and not to her Keeper for help.

I cannot risk this child's life, Ashara thought, aware that she was taking on herself the responsibilities of a Keeper. Varzil had shown her how *laran* might be permanently diverted, although he'd warned her never to try except in dire emergency.

When she'd finished, Bellisma's channels flowed as clear and steady as a child's. Now it would be a simple matter to teach her to avoid any sexual arousal, so that even a deliberately erotic caress would seem as appetizing as three-day-old porridge.

I have no choice, Ashara told herself. *Varzil would understand.*

Bellisma murmured and rolled over, instantly asleep. Smiling, Ashara stretched out beside her, and they lay together, side by side, as chaste as the moonlight.

Ashara often stayed in the laboratory after the technicians had left, checking the linkages and the unfamiliar design of the batteries. The Tower monitors insisted on examining her regularly, concerned with how little rest and food she took, but Ashara always amazed them with her continued excellent health. These days, they acted as if the entire Tower needed nursing.

Ashara had other things to worry about. Gradually the form of the device took shape and she still couldn't figure out what it was for. The *laran* batteries were strangely configured, clearly not meant for any ordinary storage function. She identified mechanisms for the transmission of a short, immensely powerful burst of energy—but for what purpose? When she asked Corus again, he put her off, nor would he say where he'd gotten the designs or for whom the project was being built.

One night Ashara sat up, poring over the diagrams for the almost-completed device. Something stirred at the back of her mind. Now that the basic construction was in place, she realized she'd seen its like somewhere before.

An image rose to her mind, from an old record from the days when the Towers served the great Domains lords, making terrible *laran* weapons for them—clingfire, bonewater dust, and more.

A weapon? Could Corus have taken a commission to build a weapon, right here in Varzil's Tower?

Ashara forced herself to calm as she gathered up the diagrams and strode along the corridor to Corus's private suite. A tendril of *laran* told her he was there, awake and alone. She knocked, and a moment later the door opened.

"Ashara, it's late," he said, standing back to let her enter. She saw, in a glance, the red, swollen channels of his lower body. What was he thinking, to allow himself to get into such a state?

"Corus, I must speak with you." She held out the plans. "I must know what this is and to what use it will be put. It's a weapon, isn't it?"

Corus turned his back on her, crossed the room and sat in his richly upholstered chair. "I knew I was taking a chance, including you on this project. I thought that once you'd settled down… Go to sleep, do your work, and leave the decisions to those who are wiser than you."

"It is a weapon," Ashara repeated evenly.

He watched her, his eyes glowering in the candlelight. "Ashara, I warn you, you have no need to know these things."

"What kind of weapon?"

Corus slammed one palm on the arm rest and got to his feet. "If I told you, what would you do with that information, eh? Whose cause would you serve? You know nothing of the world beyond the Towers. I am your Keeper, not the other way around."

"*Varzil* was my Keeper!"

Corus back-handed her across the face and sent her staggering. The surface of his mind, perhaps affected by the blocked sexual energy, seethed like a pot about to boil. Reflexively she reached out, caught a fragmentary image. Her eyes widened in shock.

A Cataclysm device, like the one that destroyed the lake at Hali.

"No!" She cried out, horror-struck. "You cannot do this! I'll warn the other Towers—"

"And who will believe you? No one else even suspects. Half the device is here, half still safe at Tramontana. And if we don't build it, someone else will, someone with no scruples about how to use it."

She got to her feet, the plans still clutched in her fist, and said stiffly, "Then I will destroy what I have built, rather than see such destruction unleashed."

"You? You're incapable of seeing sense in this matter." He stormed toward her as if he would strike her again. "You will leave this Tower immediately, watched every moment until you pass the gates. That is my command as Keeper. I will no longer tolerate your constant questioning and insubordination. If this is how Varzil trained you, then it's a good thing he's dead!"

Ashara shook with outrage as he ripped the diagrams from her fingers. Temptation flooded through her, to reach out with her Alton Gift, force his mind open before hers. It would be as terrible as any rape, against everything she believed in, everything Varzil had taught her.

But Varzil's training held firm. Ashara did not give in to her fury. She allowed herself to be escorted down to her room, where she packed her few belongings. An hour later she found herself wrapped in a travel cloak, sitting on an old white mare. The air was still, but a light sprinkling of snow covered the ground. A few clouds scudded across the night sky, glowing softly with the light of three moons.

Ashara raised her head. Corus thought he could humiliate her by packing her off in the middle of the night in total disregard for her rank and birth, without even a decent chaperone. He thought she'd go crawling back to her family and a marriage to some upstart desperate enough for an alliance with the Altons to take her.

"No," she said softly, a vow made in her heart, "I will not go back to Armida, but to Hali, where Raimond Lindir offered me a place. Whatever happens, Varzil's dream must not die!"

Numb with cold and exhaustion, Ashara stood at the gates of Hali Tower an hour after sunset. It took her a few moments to summon the strength to pull the bell rope. There had been days on the trail when only her rage at Corus MacAran and the other fools of the Tower council kept her alive and moving. She'd walked the last miles on her own feet after her mount collapsed.

Now she lifted her chin and addressed the sleepy-eyed porter. "I am Ashara Alton, under-Keeper of Neskaya Tower, and I have come to serve here at the invitation of Raimond Lindir."

The motherly woman who supervised the housekeeping bustled Ashara into a heated room, plied her with food, and settled her in bed under three feather comforters, refusing to hear a word of explanation.

As Ashara slept, her mind wandered in the gray formlessness of the Overworld. Here she felt no pain, no hunger or thirst or bone-weary fatigue. Her body seemed as light as a feather. In the distance, she saw a human figure, hauntingly familiar, moving away from her. Instantly she recognized Varzil.

It was dangerous to be abroad in the Overworld, but never more so that one was exhausted and heart-sore. Ashara longed to follow Varzil and be with him, to see his face and hear his voice one last time. If she tried, she knew, she might wander there forever. She held still by only the frailest margin of will. In desperation, she imagined herself in the midst of a blue flame, cut off from all temptation.

Walls of cold, azure fire burst into being around her, deepening in hue with each passing moment. Ashara clung to them, as if she could make herself one with their frigid beauty. An instant later, Varzil's retreating form was lost to view. She drifted back to her body.

The next morning, Raimond Lindir received Ashara formally. He commented that the roads were not safe these days, with the Hastur lords rumbling rebellion and war so close at hand. "I had not thought to welcome you so soon," he said without the slightest trace of emotion. "Neskaya's loss is Hali's gain."

"I shall strive to be worthy of that trust," she answered.

"Whatever reason Corus had for dismissing you, I cannot so lightly overlook the appearance of disobedience. You will have to earn your right to the position you formerly held. I can grant you only a technician's status."

Ashara held her face expressionless. What had she expected? And yet Raimond spoke of earning her right. So be it, then. She would show him what kind of Keeper Varzil had trained.

In the days that followed, Ashara recovered her strength and poured it gladly into whatever task was set before her. For the first time since Varzil's death, she began to think she might be happy. Raimond Lindir was a very different sort of Keeper from Corus. He didn't waste time on distracting emotions and she never caught even a whiff of sexual interest from him. It was as if he had been made *emmasca* according to the old traditions.

Ashara continued the training exercises Varzil had taught

her, often staying up very late, deep in breath-control trance. To avoid any inadvertent energy leakage, she set up a *laran* barrier around her room. One night, when she'd been at Hali Tower only a few months, she sensed nothing amiss until a voice rang out down the corridor.

Instantly alert, Ashara grabbed a thick woolen shawl and jerked her door open. Cheria, one of the young monitors, darted toward her, unbound hair streaming down her back. Her face was flushed, her eyes rounded with fright.

"Ashara!" she gasped. "Help—you must come!" With a desperate backward glance, she raced on toward the next room, sounding the alarm.

Ashara paused, reaching out with her *laran* senses. Now, with her barrier down, she felt Raimond's polished mind as he assembled the Tower into a circle.

Ashara had not gone more than a few steps down the icy corridor when a ripple of inhumanly powerful mental energy slammed her against the wall. She staggered and barely caught herself from falling.

Blessed Cassilda! She'd never in her life felt anything like that—*laran* with no taint of human personality, a warping of the basic forces that held matter together. She scrambled to her feet and raced downstairs.

His face frozen in concentration, Raimond bent over the great matrix screen which was the heart of Hali Tower. Around him, pale and eerie in its blue light, sat the two under-Keepers, technicians, and senior monitors.

Ashara slipped into place across the circle from him and clasped hands with the workers on either side.

Without warning, the psychic firmament flexed once more, as if nature itself were being uprooted. Ashara's breath was

112

squeezed from her lungs and her vision darkened. Stone walls cracked and splintered. The Tower seemed to sway on its very foundations.

With a few practiced breaths, Ashara settled her body into a trance state. For a moment she seemed to hover above Hali Tower. She looked down on it and the glimmering lake, and the village where fires had broken out and men scrambled like frantic insects to put them out. She shifted her vision; colors blurred into shadow. Neskaya Tower burned in the far distance like a torch of sorcerous flame.

A crackle of lightening shot out from Neskaya Tower in the direction of Thendara. Corus must have brought the pieces of the Cataclysm device together; he'd spoken of using it in a cause. For an instant, Ashara wished she'd paid more attention to the politics of the day. Varzil had thought them important; he'd said something about a Hastur lord at Thendara—

It didn't matter now. The lightning arched above her, swelling and branching. More and more tendrils shot out from its trunk, curving down towards the earth. Where each slender branch touched the earth, a noise like thunder rolled through the air. Rock crumbled to powder, trees and buildings to smoke.

Ashara, with her trained sensitivity, felt the collapse of the very forces binding matter together. The Cataclysm device, like a monster out of legend, seemed to gain new intensity from each disintegration.

Around her physical body came wails of terror and despair. Dimly she heard the other workers gasping, sobbing. Someone screamed and a body thudded to the floor. Only Raimond held firm, desperately trying to keep his circle together. But his *leroni* were slipping away, his own powers too weak to hold them.

Raimond! Ashara reached for him and, after a startled instant, he linked his mind with hers. She searched the Tower for those whose will and reason had not been broken by the awesome psychic forces raging overhead. She found a few—less than half—and brought them into the circle. Quickly she gathered their *laran* energies, weaving them together as she would a skein of finest silk, spinning a web of protection around the Tower.

The rumbling retreated to a muted, barely audible sound. The stone floor steadied under her feet.

"Thanks be," someone murmured. "We're safe."

The Circle began to break up. "No!" Ashara commanded. "It must be destroyed!"

"That?" Raimond stared at her, his face white, mouth stretched taut. "How? It's beyond any of our powers. I can't—"

"But *I* can!" She would have to link with other circles in other Towers, too far for ordinary *laran* to reach. But there was another way…

Ashara gathered the *laran* energy from the Hali circle and burst into the Overworld in a blaze of shimmering blue fire. Gashes of lurid red and black cut through the usually featureless gray landscape. Hills and crevices of blood-soaked dust surrounded her. To one side, Comyn Tower in Thendara writhed and shrieked as if it were a living thing. Inside, its defenders flared and died like embers. Their screams echoed through her mind.

Opposite it, Neskaya Tower blazed, spewing forth supernatural fire. Everything it touched turned to ashes and then to nothingness, worse than any clingfire. Ragged holes appeared in the very fabric of the Otherworld. Then the attack lessened, as if the device were recharging.

Ashara!

Behind her stood a young woman she instantly recognized as

the mental image of Ellimara of Corandolis Tower. She reached out her hand. Ashara took it and felt a surge of power—Ellimara and all of her circle that yet remained.

With all her inborn talent and skill, honed by desperation and years of rigorous training, Ashara visualized a circle extending the length of the Domains. She had been right to move the struggle to the Overworld, for here distance meant nothing. She found herself surrounded by human forms, some solid, others flickering and insubstantial.

With a Keeper's firm touch, she brought them all into the circle: Arilinn, Nevarsin, far Dalereuth, and Tramontana. Even Mikhail at Comyn Tower answered her. The next instant, they stood, hands and minds joined, around the inferno that had been Neskaya. With a quick, sure touch, she shaped their forces into a net, then a blanket, and cast it over the Tower.

For a moment nothing happened, then Neskaya erupted in an explosion of raging, mindless energy. It seared Ashara's psychic form and threatened to blast through the shield. Ashara tensed, but her circle held.

Suddenly she felt the shift in the device's focus. No longer was its destructive force directed at Thendara, it was now aimed directly at her circle.

The foundation of the Overworld quivered like a living thing and the blanket that Ashara had visualized began to tear and shred. Promontories of flame burst through it, leaping into jagged white lightning as they rampaged outward.

Hold! Ashara cried, as the fabric of the blanket disintegrated into tatters. Fire raced along the circle, seizing the men and women. Their psychic bodies blurred until all Ashara could see was a skeleton outline of their glowing *laran* channels.

Screams pierced the air, cries of stark agony. Arnad of

Arilinn winked out of sight, his aged heart unable to withstand the strain. Mikhail of Comyn Tower arched backwards, his psychic body laced with red like molten metal. Something deep within him exploded. His body blew apart into scraps of ashes.

Ashara desperately tried to reform her circle. Not even Varzil himself would have had the power to hold them together. But the next instant, a pattern leapt to her mind. Around her, some *leroni* struggled and died while others continued, strong but fewer each passing moment. The key was right in front of her: the pulsing red sexual energy blocking their channels. The Cataclysm device was somehow attuned to that energy, perhaps a bizarre reversal of the process of life creation. Every sexually active man or woman who'd worked on it and now battled it was drawn into its perverted pattern.

Only I can withstand it, Ashara realized. *I and others like me.*

Instantly she sorted through the giant circle, seeking those workers who, through training or personal choice, had remained chaste. Their minds joined hers in a blaze like purest blue fire. She formed the energy into walls of solid, impenetrable ice, blocking the Cataclysm device's lightning on every side.

Moment after moment, the fire grew less fierce. Then a tremendous explosion racked the Overworld, contained within the blue ice crystal of Ashara's circle, and gradually died away into silence.

Days later, Ashara awoke, shivering, in her room in Hali Tower. Cheria, the young monitor, bent over her with an anxious expression. Ashara sat up and tried to speak. She was too exhausted to form words, too exhausted to reach out with her *laran*. But not too exhausted to realize that of all the Keepers on Darkover, all that remained were Ellimara of Corandolis, part-*chieri* Raimond Lindir, and herself.

The other Towers did not argue for long, even what was left of Neskaya. The choice was to accept Ashara's terms or their own slow death. They could limp by for only a few years with their under-Keepers, doing mostly low-level work. It would take far longer for the widespread destruction of the Cataclysm device, even contained as it was, to be reversed.

"I will train your new Keepers," Ashara told them, "but I will train them in my own way." They had all agreed to send her their best novices—young girls only, as she demanded.

But, Ashara reminded herself, the memories of men were as short as their gratitude. Look at how quickly they'd abandoned Varzil's teachings, when it was expedient to do so.

I will not allow that to happen again. Varzil might die and be forgotten, but I will not!

She would train virgin Keepers for as long as she was able, and after that, she would build a new Tower in Thendara. Ashara's Tower. From there, she would find a way for the work to continue until no one dared question her methods.

She could not know it would take the death of Cleindori Aillard, hundreds of years in the future, to reverse the harm she would do.

The White *Oudrakhi*

T he day that had begun so auspiciously was about to end in disaster. Haned eyed the setting ruby sun with a mixture of resentment and exasperation, pulling the dun *oudrakhi* to a sloppy, ill-balanced halt. The animal dodged the cuff aimed at its delicate, fan-shaped ears and hissed back in temper. The man controlled himself with an effort. There was no point in abusing the beast just because it could not climb the steepening foothills in the dark.

Haned swept a straggle of blond hair from his eyes as if the gesture itself would give him a better view of the trail in the failing light. His cold-numbed muscles ached to return home to his pregnant wife or at very least camp here on level ground sheltered by the *oudrakhi*'s warm body. Yet he could not, could *not* in the face of all senselessness force himself to abandon the chase. Tonight he ought to be celebrating the prophecy of twin sons and toasting his best sale of premium riding animals, yet here he was, half-frozen and closer to the witch-ridden Domains than any sane man ought to venture, chasing one lone wayward white *oudrakhi*.

The hold the beast had on him, ever since the two had been lost in a storm in these very hills, passed all belief. He had even considered selling the white *oudrakhi* just to rid his *kihar* of the taint of dependence, but at the last could not bring himself to do it. Gradually his unmanly terror of their separation had ripened into the seething fury that filled his guts tonight.

Cursing at the injustice of it all, he unsaddled and hobbled his present steed, the young gelded male whose speed and easy gait almost compensated for its nasty temper and lack of intelligence. A few sweeps for dry brush gave him the makings for a marker fire. The young animal lowered itself awkwardly to the ground as its master took a long cloak from the saddle packs and began to climb.

Fortune favored him with a token as he bent lower to focus on the tracks. Two of Darkover's four moons shone brightly in the night sky, with a third to rise soon. Skills learned during his boyhood years of tracking errant beasts from his father's herds would pay extra dividends tonight. Like deliberate signs for him to follow, the *oudrakhi*'s distinctive hoof prints practically shone in the dusk. Haned soon fell into a smooth rhythm of search and climb.

As he went he tried to cheer himself with thoughts of the brighter moments of the day, yet the anxiety he always felt in the absence of the white *oudrakhi* spoiled even this small pleasure for him. He let his thoughts dwell on the pride of his two future sons, only to gradually descend into doubt of the seer's words—after all, who could be positive about a thing like that?—and besides, the boys were like enough to make a mess of the *oudrakhi* breeding farm he and his father had built up, if they weren't seduced into running away to those *Terranan* first.

Then he thought of the sale he had made that day, the best prices he had yet gotten for *oudrakhi* of his own breeding and training. Soon he was deep in worry as to whether he should not have kept some of the animals as breeding stock and if that one gray female was indeed broken of kicking while being mounted. Since her disposition was otherwise flawless and her confirmation excellent, he had sold her as a lady's mount, and now visions of mangled consorts of dangerously powerful men assaulted him. He might face the dubious future of an eventual *kifurgh* challenge.

By this time he had reached the crest of the first line of hills and was able to look down to steepness to the uncomfortably small orange dot of his marker fire. For an instant Haned allowed himself to be tempted into returning and even went so far as to take a few steps downslope before the familiar sick twisting in his head forced him back to the *oudrakhi*'s trail. It seemed there was no escaping his tie with the animal, a thought that did little to sweeten his disposition.

He traveled down into a shallow dell, then toiled up the next ridge and around the crevasse, onward and upward while the moons spun their dance through the starry fields. As he climbed higher, the sickness within him eased somewhat and his usual cheerful thoughts began to reappear. It was not so bad to be alone in the quiet, dark hills; as a boy he had once camped higher than this on a dare from his knife-brother. He was warm enough under his cloak woven by his wife from the soft winter coats of his own *oudrakhi*. His wife, now there was a subject worth warming to...

The twisting feeling lightened suddenly and Haned knew he was close to the runaway. He stepped into a cup of soft grasses, bright enough with moonlight so that he could easily see the silver sheen of the *oudrakhi*'s coat as it scrambled to its feet and ambled toward him.

Relief like a tight knot loosening swept through him as the

oudrakhi nuzzled him with most un-*oudrakhi*-like affection and whuffled softly in its own language. *Such an animal, such a silky coat, almost luminous in the pale light,* Haned thought. It was no wonder he prized it so highly as to chase into these frigid hills at night.

A sudden noise, the click of a leather heel on stone, brought Haned to alarmed attention. He whipped out the saber that never left his side outside of his own house and peered through the dark.

A light voice called out in lilting *casta*, which he recognized but did not understand. *A Domains woman, here in these hills!* The bright flare of a small hand-carried lamp flashed as its bearer stepped from behind a boulder, then another, until he could distinguish six people including the woman, Domains dwellers all. Although there had been peace between the Dry Towns and their neighbors since he could remember, Haned tightened his grasp on the handle of his saber and flexed his thighs into a fighting stance.

"We come in peace to all of the Dry Towns," one of the men called out in *cahuenga*. The lamplight could not disguise his aristocratic features or the flaming brilliance of the woman's hair.

"I hear you," Haned answered in a *cahuenga*, grateful to his elder sister, who had cajoled their father into teaching and both of them a second language before being handed to her new husband in Carthon.

"It's him; it's got to be him," said the woman in the same language.

"But, Lady Linnea, he's a Dry Towner," protested one of the men.

"So were the Ridenow," she replied with quiet authority.

"Dani, you'd better talk to him."

The man who had first hailed Haned stepped to the fore of the group, empty hands well away from his strange straight sword. "We greet you not as Domains to Dry Towns but as one a citizen of Darkover to another. We of the Telepath Council appeal to you to join us and help to mend and strengthen our world."

Haned could not restrain a blink of disbelief at this outrageous plea. If the man had the wit to recognize the rudeness, however, he did not respond. Curious as to the extent of this madness, Haned unbent enough to lower the tip of his saber.

"Very well, I will listen," he said politely.

"You have heard of the *Terranan* from the stars?"

Haned grunted. "In my father's time such stories were thought to be but ravings, yet I myself have seen these *Terranan* come to trade for pelts and medicinal herbs." He did not add that, in his opinion, the *Terranan* had no notion of how to bargain for anything and if they paid prices so high as to be indecent, it was their own fault. If the Domains did not already know the *Terranan* to be fools, Haned was not going to enlighten them.

"For generations we have resisted their efforts to make Darkover only another watering hole, part of their vast Empire, yet times change. The Comyn must change also. To remain separate and yet strong, we must call on all our resources, wherever we find them. Our most precious asset is people like you."

So these were some of the legendary witches Haned had heard child-stories about. He peered more closely at them, but the lamp and the moonlight showed only handsome, regular features with a tint of red hair in the man and the fiery brilliance of the woman's braided crown.

"We are searching for any who possess the special abilities we call *laran*," the man said. "We monitored yours from a distance and were able to follow your starstone here."

"Are you saying I am a witch, too?" he muttered in disbelief.

"No, nothing so superstitious," the woman burst out impatiently. "This is science, not magic."

Haned glowered the impudent, unchained wench into silence as the young man quickly continued. "We know you have *laran* because we were able to trace your starstone."

"Starstone, you keep saying starstone! I know of no such thing!"

The young Domains lord glanced in doubt at the woman. "Linnea?"

"He's keyed into one, all the same, and it's here," she insisted.

"Show me this starstone you claim is proof of my witchhood," growled Haned, now feeling confused and a little frightened but adamant that his *kihar* should not suffer publicly because of it.

The woman took a small amulet from the neck of her gown and slowly unwrapped it, cupping it like a precious thing in her six-fingered hands. Haned thought he saw a flash of blue as she covered it, closing her eyes. "It's *in* that *oudrakhi*," she whispered.

"I don't believe you," exclaimed Haned. "You claim I'm a witch and I must go help you because of something you say my *oudrakhi* ate? What kind of a fool do you take me for?"

"No fool at all," replied the young lord, "but a man of fairness. Let us prove it to you."

Haned nodded and watched the woman, still cupping her amulet, move closer to the *oudrakhi*, murmuring softly to the beast. Although usually temperamental around strangers, the animal stood calmly as she approached it; then suddenly arched its back, snapping at its silvery flanks as if in pain.

"Colic!" Haned swore. "You've witched my beast into sickness!"

"No. Watch."

The *oudrakhi* lowered its head between its callused knees as a series of spasmodic contractions passed through its body, then quickly vomited a pile of partially digested grasses, pebbles, and a single gleaming blue jewel.

Haned, his palms sweating, kept his grip on his saber as he knelt to touch the stone. It felt surprisingly hot to the touch, although he told himself that anything that had lain in the belly of an *oudrakhi* would be warm. A wave of inner comfort passed through him as he closed his fingers around it.

"You see," said the nobleman. "That's a matrix, a special stone to focus *laran*, and it's clearly yours. Don't you feel how it's attuned to you? That means you've keyed into it, which proves you have *laran*. We appeal to you, join us and learn to use it. The work is hard, but you'll live as one of us in Thendara and all of Darkover will honor you."

Haned turned away, warmed by the flood of sensation from the blue jewel. His mind raced along the possibilities. If this crystal had been the cause of his unnatural attachment to the white *oudrakhi*, then he held in his own hand the means to his freedom, his return to perfect independence. Yet he could not just hoard the gem for the sake of his own selfish pride, and he knew he could not learn to use it without help. If what these lordly people told him were true, he also held the key to a life fabulous beyond his dreams. Boyhood visions of distant mountain castles, rare treasures, and adventures tantalized him.

The *oudrakhi* had resumed a more normal posture, spitting in distaste at its undignified treatment. It staggered a few steps to its master and laid its bony head on his shoulder, blowing across his cheek and sighing a complaint. Its scent filled his nostrils, carrying memories of the herds in their corrals, sunrise in the dry fields, sweat and saddle leather.

Haned closed his eyes and saw himself garbed in one of those strange bright cloaks, walking through snow in the high mountains, his wife chainless beside him, the twins growing up strangers to the back of an *oudrakhi*. The vision swept through him with a sudden chill of loss. Who would he be in those mystic, translucent castles, ripped from the herds and deserts that had birthed him? No longer Dry Towner, never Domains dweller, then what? Was this the price of perfect freedom and adventure? And the fate of Darkover that the young nobleman had pleaded for, did that too rest upon his exile?

"You'll join us, won't you? We can offer you much more than your life here," the young man was repeating.

Haned's vision cleared like haze burning off with sunrise, leaving only the dew glittering on the sands. Where was his *kihar* now, in the palm of his hand with the blue starstone, encased in the fragile flesh of the *oudrakhi*, or inherent in the very stuff of his life?

The white *oudrakhi* regarded him with dark, enigmatic eyes, as solid and capricious as the mountain under his feet, the perfect setting for the blue jewel. Haned seized the soft nose of the beast, thrust of the starstone down its gullet, and felt it swallow reflexively. Then he vaulted to its back and looked down at the startled Domains party.

"Your pardon, gentles," he said, unaccustomed emotion often in his voice, "but I will not go with you to learn this *laran* at the price of my own *kihar*. All the starstones in Darkover cannot turn a backwoods *oudrakhi* herder into a high Comyn lord, and if they could, what would be left worth defending from the *Terranan*? Besides," he grinned crookedly, "it's just too damn cold in these mountains for the likes of me."

The *oudrakhi* leapt in response to its master's commands, flicking its short, feathery tail as Haned directed it with voice and heels down the path toward his camp. The nobleman and the red-haired woman exchanged astonished glances.

"Did he mean he *wanted* to keep herding those smelly beasts?"

"I don't know, Dani. I've often heard it said that there's no understanding a *cralmac* or a Dry Towner. Now I believe it."

The Carthon Connection

M any years ago in a fine estate on the outskirts of Shainsa
lived a copper trader, Senth by name, who had nine
wives. A harsh man was he, and so fiercely jealous of his *kihar*
that he would as soon drench the sands with his own blood as
quiver one instant before an affront. His coffers bulged with the
riches of his trade, but his heart was empty for although his
wives brought forth daughter after daughter, he had no son to
carry on his name.

The youngest of Senth's wives was a tender lady named
Ramira, who within a year of her marriage grew big-bellied and
fruitful after the fashion of newly wedded wives. When at last
her time came, for two days and two nights she labored to bring
forth her child, and not a kind word or a soft glance did Senth
bestow upon her for all those weary hours. Senth's first wife, the
Lady Calla, tended Ramira as tenderly as her own daughter,
remaining at her side throughout her ordeal, for Ramira had
touched her heart with her generosity and gentleness.

At last the babe was born, and great joy spread throughout
the house, for it was the long-awaited son. Alas, no sooner had
Senth burst into the lady's room and, bristly with fierceness,
snatched up his child, than the baby gave a thin, mewling cry

and perished upon the spot.

Wrath and despair flooded across the face of Senth. His fists trembled as he put the bundle down and towered above his youngest wife. He bellowed loudly enough to waken the faraway lords of the Domains, "Witch! Foul and bloody witch! You have stolen my son from me! Worthless piece of baggage, that I ever wasted my seed upon you!" Then he cursed her most vilely in a voice that the entire household could hear her shame. At last he left her, so stunned and bereaved that she could not weep. In the darkness, her sister-wives gathered round to comfort her as best they could.

The worst was yet to come, for the next morning, before the great red sun had cleared the horizon, Senth once again strode into the lady's chamber and dragged her to her feet.

"Do you think you are more than an unworthy possession, that you can flaunt your master's wishes in this manner?" he stormed.

"I have always tried my best to please you in all things, O my husband," Ramira replied in a meek voice.

"Husband no more!" he roared, and stripped her of her chains. Then he picked her up, slung her over his shoulders like a sack of uncombed linex, and carried her into the nearby market square. There he flung her down, spitting upon her and saying, "Whoever is stupid enough to want you may have you," and departed.

Ramira lay there in the dusty square, chainless and shocked, with nothing but the robes she now wore. Grief filled her for the loss of her child, her first child that she had carried beneath her beating heart, had sung to, had longed for, now gone as if he had never existed. Her full breasts ached beneath the bindings that Lady Calla had applied the night before, yet the pain of her body was a shadow beside the pain of her heart. She huddled on the dusty ground for a long time, rocking gently and crooning to herself. As the day wore on, fruit sellers, cloth dealers, and merchants of all varieties filled the market, but she lay as if dumb and blind.

Finally Ramira looked up to see Old Elvira, the town beggar, crouched beside her. Elvira with her one yellowed tooth, her hump, and her scuttling crawl, touched her gently on the sleeve. Ramira could see on the bony wrist the long-faded scars where once the chains of wifehood had rested. That was long ago, and now no man would own Old Elvira; she was simply hideous and worthless. Ramira had pitied her and given her a few coins for water and a grain wafer from time to time.

"Naw, ye cain't stay here, young miss, indeed," drawled the crone as she urged Ramira to her feet.

"I don't understand."

"Aye and just think what a fine and toothsome lass as yerself might be doing abroad and chainless," Elvira whispered so that no passer-by might overhear.

Ramira glanced down with dismay upon her naked wrists, for the full impact of her masterless condition had not been clear to her earlier. "Oh, Elvira! I don't belong to him anymore!"

"Nor to any man, if luck be with ye, although ye may not see it for the blessing it is for many a year." The beggar woman urged her towards the communal well. "Now listen well, my sweetie, for ye know full well that a woman w'out chains is an insult to the decency of them what call themselves men. Now, naw," for Ramira had hung her head in shame, "I know it was no fault of yer own; news travels fast. Be that as it may," now they had reached the well, and the younger woman sank gratefully down beside the cool, moist wall. "Be that as it may, ye run a terrible risk, for Kobol the Whoremaster is rumored to be passin' through today. If he sees ye chainless, he'll as soon snatch ye up as sneeze at ye, and then it's away to Ardcarran with ye to die chained to the wall of some filthy brothel."

"O heavenly—" began Ramira, her eyes wide with horror.

Old Elvira hushed her with a gesture, her bright eyes darting about the square. Her bony fingers bit into Ramira's shoulder. "Aye, there he be, lass, that fat scoundrel all in yellow, greasy like the trade he follows. Quickly, lass, bury yer hands in yer lap so he cann' see whether ye'r chained or no, an' hang yer head to hide yer face. I'll draw him off so he cann' get a good look at ye."

"Elvira, I—"

"Hush, lass. An' good fortune follow thee." With those words, the old crone scuttled away, heading through the colorful, milling crowd slantwise across the square to intersect a bold-striding, garishly attired fellow, his brassy hair gleaming in the sun.

Nearing him, she set up such a racket of pleading, shouting, whining, and cursing, now tugging at the hem of his tunic and then away in a flash to escape his quick retort, until his every attention was taken up by trying to escape from her odious attentions without overly compromising his dignity. In this way, Kobol the Whoremaster passed from the village square without so much as a second glance at the young woman who sat shivering by the well.

Ramira watched the scoundrel depart, giving silent thanks to Old Elvira for her deliverance. Now dread seeped into her every fiber, for she better realized her danger.

What shall I do? Where shall I go? she wondered. Now that her husband had cast her out, neither would her kin—who had sold her to such a brute in the first place—give her solace.

She began to assess her situation, for although by nature gentle she was also practical. *Alas, I have naught but these thin robes, and they not of the best quality, a silver chain with a copper ornament—and small price that would fetch even if I could sell it safely and not be robbed—and my wits.*

Then she felt tremendously thirsty, but even though she sat at the foot of the well, she dared not drink. She lacked the coin to pay for the water and the penalty for water theft was terrible. So despair once again descended upon her.

As Ramira sat in desolation, another woman approached the well, water jug balanced gracefully on her head, jeweled chains chiming musically. Ramira looked up at the scent of the perfume as the woman bent to put down the water-price, for it was her girlhood friend and companion, Malia.

"My poor darling! That ever this should come to pass," cried the lady. "Art thirsty? Hungry?"

Ramira nodded soundlessly, and her friend pressed a cup of well water into her trembling hands, steadying it so she could drink. Then Malia dropped a packet of food and another of healing herbs into her lap, along with a few coins, saying, "I am sorry I could not bring thee more, but it would be missed."

"Thou should not even speak to me here, my dear," said Ramira, her eyes filling with tears of love and shame. "My husband has taken back his chains and I am cast out."

"Men may spit upon thee, but their scorn will never change a woman's heart, or my love for thee," returned her friend. "But I bring thee a greater gift still. Rest well through the heat of the day and strengthen thy heart, for help shall come to thee." With these words she turned, water jug sloshing with the sound of her chains. The faint scent of flowers filled Ramira's heart as much as the food and drink filled her belly.

Throughout the long day she waited by the well, watching the buyers and sellers, drinking when she had thirst, eating the good herbs soaked in well water and the strengthening food given to her. Towards dusk more women came to the well, each with a kind word for her plight and never a hard glance. Her heart filled with wonder and she thought, *All my life I have been taught that women are fit for no more than bearing sons and working hard for the man who bestows his chains upon them. But now it seems that the kindness and thoughtfulness of one of these women is a jewel worth more than the* kihar *of all the men of Shainsa.*

Just as the red sun dipped to kiss the horizon, a lone woman, heavily veiled, floated across the market square to the well. In the rapidly falling darkness she knelt by Ramira's side and drew aside her coverings.

"My lady Calla! Have you come to aid me or to revel in my shame? Surely you of all women have cause to hate me for a younger wife trying to take your place. Do you think I was unworthy of my chains?"

"Do not say so, my daughter-wife," said Lady Calla. "You must be sorely tried to think such a thing. I know only too well how little you deserved this treatment. We all sorrow for your pain, but rejoice that perhaps with courage you may find your way to a better life."

"Where can I go, O my mother-wife? All here know me, and those who would help me cannot, for fear of their husbands or fathers. Today I have been fed and comforted by my childhood friend, but who will dare to be my friend tomorrow?"

"There are many who dare, but we do not shout our secrets to the winds. But for now, how fare you? Could you travel tomorrow?"

"I do well enough, mother-wife, although I still have great thirst. I have eaten herbs to stop my bleeding, and they have given me some small measure of strength. As for traveling, I do not know where I might go."

"At dawn, present yourself at the eastern gate. A caravaneer, one Beckold, will expect you. You will know him by his great mustaches and the purple sash he always wears. I have arranged for him to take you as a gift to the wife of a man in Carthon. Mayhap you will find good fortune along the way, or escape to the Domains and take service there, or at worst come to your destination, where at least you will be justly treated." Calla drew forth a plain, unembellished set of chains, a key in the lock. "Here, with these you can travel more safely, and with the key you can shed them if need be."

With these words the elder wife helped Ramira to don the chains and then embraced her with great tenderness.

"I am not sure I welcome these," murmured Ramira, "although only a few hours ago I would have been desperate for chains once again, as if I had lost my womanhood with my bondage. Tell me, O my mother-wife, if you are so clever as to be able to arrange my escape, why do you not plan one for yourself? You cannot delight in the company of S—of that man."

Lady Calla sat back on her heels, and the pale torchlight from the nearest building lit her tired face. "No, although my life there no longer torments me as once it did. After all, Senth could scarcely run his household without me. The reason is that if I am *not* here, who would help you and others like you? So I stay, and use my position as first wife of a wealthy trader to give my life meaning."

Ramira clasped Calla's hands and held her breast-to-breast as a true sister. The warmth of Calla's courage warmed her the whole night long.

Dawn found Ramira able to walk, and so she made her way to the eastern gate. After a time, she spied a great caravan passing by the outskirts, with *oudrakhi* heavily laden with goods and guards sporting gleaming, curved blades. One beast, a fine riding animal, came towards her. As it neared, she saw the rider was as Calla had described: mustached and girded in purple.

"Ah, the baggage." The rider grunted, mostly to himself. She cast her eyes to the sand as he inspected her, wheeling his *oudrakhi* in a circle. "Well, you may wash up presentable," he said, "but you can't travel in those rags. I've better in my pack, but it'll cost your mistress extra. Up with you now," and he swung her behind him and carried her off.

Beckold the caravaneer proved to be a man rough but not cruel, loud-laughing with his men and careful with his *oudrakhi*. He garbed Ramira in robes and veils suitable for travel and set her apart on her own riding animal. Later he gave her coarse, adequate food and drink but spoke little to her.

Although the travel pace wore wearily upon her the first few days she complained not but fixed her eyes and hopes on the far-off line of hills that marked Carthon. The guards eyed her curiously and left her alone when Beckold glared at them. So, after many a long day, they came into sight of the city of Carthon, where Dry Towner and Domainer lived in uneasy peace.

A half day's journey from the city gates, the caravan was

beset by a small, swiftly mounted band. They rode small horses, strange beasts from the Domains, and brandished straight swords and colorful, swirling capes. The *oudrakhi* that Ramira bestrode went berserk with the confusion and smell of the new animals, tearing away from the caravan. Terrified though she was, Ramira clung to its back, thinking that death might be better than capture by bandits and untold new horrors. Her mount, unused to the rough, scrubby terrain, stumbled and fell with a hoarse cry, and over its head she sailed, striking her head and embracing blackness.

When at last she woke, a new sun was rising and the air was sweet with the scent of spicebush and the songs of birds. Ramira brushed the dust off her robes, shook loose her veils, and looked around her. No trace remained of the *oudrakhi*, the caravan, or the bandits, but Carthon loomed nearer than before.

Fortune has indeed favored me, she thought. *I must have lain unnoticed by trader or ruffian, and now may come to this new city free to choose my own fate.* She trembled as she removed her chains. *I may be seized for a masterless woman and chained again, in which case I shall me no worse off, but I have heard that a woman may go unfettered in the Domains, and that is worth the risk. When first I took on the chains of womanhood, I thought they would bring me happiness and fulfillment, but instead I found only cruelty and disgrace.* She spat upon her chains as she left them in the dust.

Ramira rested on her way to Carthon, for although the days of the caravan had hardened her as all her years in cloistered gardens had not, the way was still long. She held her head high as she entered the gates, looking in wonder at the variety of people who thronged the streets.

A wealth of new sights assailed her eyes: dark-complexioned men and unchained women in outlandish, bright colors, beasts of many kinds from *oudrakhi* to chervines, wonderful scents and, rising above it all like a drapery in the sky, the snow-wrapped Hellers.

Ramira leaned against a post of wood instead of the familiar stone to gaze upon the heights. Like most Dry Towners, she had scoffed at tales of the mountains, and now felt herself small and insignificant in their shadow. The smell of freshly baked nut-bread sent rumblings of hunger through her belly. A woman, strangely garbed in tartan, was setting out small loaves and buns smelling of roasted meat on a white-clothed trading table.

The woman looked up to meet Ramira's gaze, red highlights gleaming amid the gray in her braided hair. She smiled and Ramira took a step towards her, stumbling as weariness swept over her.

"You poor child," clucked the woman in heavily accented but understandable *cahuenga*. She encircled Ramira in her strong arms and led her within the shop to a padded bench. "You look exhausted! Where is your family, to let you wander around half-dead like this?"

"I have no family," murmured Ramira, shaping each word carefully so that she might be understood.

"Ah!" breathed the woman. "You're from the Dry Towns. Shainsa?" Ramira nodded. "You'd best come within, then," and led her behind an embroidered drapery to a small back room, roughly furnished in wooden furniture but very clean. With a sigh Ramira sank down on the indicated low bed, her nostrils filling with the scent of fresh herbs arising from the bedding. The woman fussed over her, bustled out, and returned with a platter of meat rolls and dried fruit, a pitcher of water, and a mug of steaming dark liquid.

"Now drink the *jaco* while it's hot, and if you want any more to eat, or you need help, call out and I'll hear you. I'm Anya, by the by, and I run this bakery with the sometimes help of my good man, Piedro. I'll be in the outer shop, until this round of baking is sold, and then I'll close up." She departed in a swirl of skirts.

Obediently Ramira downed the bitter *jaco* and meat rolls, although the fruit was too sweet for her taste. Many hours she slept, and when she awakened her new friend bathed her and dressed her in the fashion of the Hellers.

Slowly Ramira told her story, and Anya listened intently. Later, Piedro appeared, a swarthy, quiet man all in greens and browns, who grunted when Anya introduced Ramira as her far kinswoman. Nor did Ramira ever hear him speak more than a few words.

Ramira found a friend and a position at the bakery on her first day in Carthon. Days passed and she learned to work at Anya's side—for Piedro did little of the actual work. Anya presented her as the cousin of her second sister-in-law, who had lived in a group marriage with a man of the Dry Towns, and to Ramira's surprise, no one asked further once they heard she had lost a child and her husband. She thought to keep her own company, avoiding the Dry Towners who dwelt in Carthon, but the cheer and friendliness of the Domains women slowly drew her out. She listened to tales of sorcerers and kings, of lakes of cloud and towers of magic, and at last she heard of the free women of the Domains, the *Comhi letzii* or Free Amazons.

"It is the one chance a woman has to be on her own, apart

from husband, father, brother, or lord," said Anya with a rare trace of envy.

"How do they live, then?" Ramira asked.

"As any honest person does: trader, guide, soldier, or even," Anya said with a smile, "baker. It is not the occupation that makes a woman free, but her own courage and determination. Yet it is not an easy life, for they are often thought a disgrace, although their honesty commands respect."

"I have found that neither hardship nor disgrace could keep a woman from doing what was needful," said Ramira, lowering her gaze. "Yet I do not know if renouncing the society of men is the pathway to happiness for all women."

"Ah," replied Anya, a knowing gleam in her eyes. "You speak of your own desires, and of Daniskar the harness maker who has been leaving flowers and pretty pebbles outside your window."

Ramira blushed like a new bride. "It is a new thing for me to have a man seek to please me, for no man in the Dry Towns—at least, no man that I ever knew—would think to do so. Malia says that her husband is generous and loving at home, she says—" She broke off as a spasm of homesickness and longing passed through her. Tears rose unbidden to her eyes for the loving friends she had lost.

"My dear," said Anya gently, "is it not the same everywhere, that some men are kind and others cruel, some women shallow and others courageous? The love and loyalty you shared cannot be cancelled out by the evil that nearly destroyed you."

"No, I suppose not. Daniskar is attentive and polite. The first time he called me *mestra*, I could not believe he meant me! He stood there, cap in hand, for longer than it would take to knead a batch of nut-bread, trying to ask me for permission to call again. I wonder he did not beg from Piedro first!" Her tears cleared in a fond smile.

"Oh, he did, in a way, through me, as it is no secret who makes the decisions in this household. I told him you were above the age of consent and could do as you wished."

"But can I really, Anya? You have taught me much about the Domains and how customs hold here in Carthon, but not how a woman can truly be her own mistress."

"Yes, it seems there is always some man or other to answer to, whether he be husband, father, or liege-lord. Perhaps it is only a matter of degree." She caught Ramira's eyes with a knowing, secret gaze. "There are many bold and daring things a woman may accomplish if she does not shout her secrets from the battlements."

Ramira nodded in understanding, for she knew that Anya had received word of her coming and had looked for her. Anya had taught her the hidden ways that messages might be sent, had introduced her to other links in the chain, including the Dry Towner woman she had been sent to.

Autumn melted into winter, bringing a fierce, icy cold that Ramira had never before experienced. She bundled up in the heavy, colorful shawls and skirts Anya gave her and strode out in the bright snow. More often than by happenstance, Daniskar the harness maker would be abroad on those mornings and would walk with her awhile. At Midwinter, she found a bunch of ice-blossoms tied with a blue ribbon on her doorstep, and thereafter she wore the ribbon on her outings.

In the dead of winter, Piedro fell ill from a lung fever.

Although Anya and Ramira nursed him carefully, he died within a tenday. Sadly they packed his body in ice to bury in the spring. For many a tenday thereafter, Anya went about her work quiet and pensive, and when asked would say little about her troubles.

"I am trying to determine if this is the proper time for a decision," was all she would tell Ramira.

Finally the spring thaw loosened winter's hold upon Carthon, muddying the streets and sending forth explosions of flowers. Sometimes Ramira's doorstep was littered with blossoms. Piedro was buried in the newly softened soil with all due ceremony, attended by most of the Domains folk of the city.

As the people filed by to pay their formal respects, Ramira was struck by the warmth of so many of them. For the first time, she felt she belonged here, when less than a year ago she had been a stranger.

Daniskar stayed after the rest of the mourners had left. "*Mestra* Ramira," he said in his low, careful voice. "Might I walk with you?"

Ramira nodded, smiling. "I would be glad of your company."

After they went on a time in silence, he stopped and took her mittened hand in his. "I am no harpsmith to be handy with words, but I must speak wheat is in my heart. Surely you must know what I–how I have–come to feel for you. And you have never turned me away or had harsh words for me, so I hoped you might care for me as well."

Ramira stood very still, unable to think of what to say, how to answer his quickening rush of words.

"Now that old Piedro is buried, I mean with spring coming on, there will be plantings and births, and weddings, too. I was hoping–was wondering if you and I might be wed." He stopped awkwardly, his eyes alight with hope and embarrassment.

Ramira jerked her hand away. "I don't–I mean, I was married before."

"Aye, so *Mestra* Anya said. But we are not Comyn here, to marry *di catenas* forever. If you husband is dead or–lost, by our laws you are still free to marry as a freemate," he pleaded, "if you wish it."

"And you still want me, knowing I have belonged to another man?" said Ramira.

"I would want you even if–even if, ach! I do not know what! But I will be a good and faithful husband to you, truly I will. I am not rich, but whatever I have shall be yours. I do not gamble or drink my earnings as so other men do." His eyes fell. "But if perhaps there is some other you favor, I must have my answer."

"No, no, it is not that," she replied. "I like you well enough, and I am sure you would be a good husband. It is–well, I never thought to marry again. I must think this through." She smiled up at him shyly. "You must give me time to make a good decision."

He relaxed with a breath. "Oh, *mestra*, I would wait for you as long as you wish, if I have reason to hope."

In the days that followed, Ramira thought long and hard about Daniskar's proposal. Her family had cared nothing for her own feelings and preferences when they made her first marriage, and never had she thought to be able to choose the path of her own life. One evening she went to Anya for counsel.

"I do not know if I love him," she said. "He is not particularly handsome, but he is kind and has tried hard to please me. I do not believe he will become a tyrant once we are wed."

"No, I do not think so, either, and I have known him since he was a child. What holds you back, then?"

"The goodness of my life here," Ramira said.

"I do not wish to push you into the arms of any man, but I too have come to a decision. I could stay here, run the bakery, and probably be pressured into marrying again, but all my life I have longed for a different sort of adventure. Now I have resolved to take the freedom that the gods have given me. The mountain passes will soon be open and I mean to journey to Thendara and join the Guild of Free Amazons."

Ramira stared at her, mouth open.

"Oh, sister!" said Anya. "Come with me! It will mean freedom for us both. We can go where we will without the need of a husband for protection, or his permission. Perhaps we could set up our own bakery in Thendara. Say you will come!"

Ramira looked down at her work-worn hands, her wrists innocent of chains. "If you are leaving Carthon, who will look out for another such as I?"

"That question has disturbed me, I admit. But in the end, I see that I have spent my whole life serving others—my father, my husband, my sisters. I am no longer young, and my spirit longs to be free. I want to live my own life while I still can. You need not wait so long; you have another choice besides a marriage with Daniskar. Come with me to Thendara!"

Ramira looked up, tears stinging her eyes. She clasped Anya to her. "O my sister, I thank you, for now I see what I must do. Here in Carthon I have been happier than ever before in my life, but I would be dead and dust were it not for the courage and love of my sisters. Calla said that her life had meaning instead of selfishness because she chose service instead of freedom. She and Old Elvira and my dear friend, Malia, all risked so much to help me, and it is to them that I owe my service now.

"And so, my dear sister, I will stay in Carthon and marry Daniskar, although part of my heart will go with you to Thendara and freedom. You have taught me much: how to live in Carthon and love its people, and of the message-ways of women throughout Darkover. In return, my sister-gift to you is that you may follow your dream with an easy mind, knowing that your post here will not be empty. I will take your place and help others."

The two embraced and wept in love and farewell.

Anya stayed in Carthon for Ramira's freemate wedding, then sold the bakery and traveled over the mountains to the Thendara Guildhouse. From time to time, a trader would bring a message from the Free Amazon Anya n'ha Mikka to the house of Ramira, wife of the harness maker. Although they never met again, their hearts were linked, and each found peace and joy in her own way.

I wrote this story in 1988 as a birthday gift for Marion and sent it to her with the words, *"Here is a tale for your delight."* Its inspiration came from her guidelines for *Four Moons of Darkover*, in which she listed unacceptable topics: no women yearning to be dominated (as in the *Gor* novels of John Norman, which at that time were also published by DAW), no resurrecting Dorilys of *Stormqueen*, and no impossibilities…like a heat wave in the Hellers. I tried to incorporate as many of these "no-no's" as I could. At the time, I had never had a serious discussion with a transgender person, let alone acquired a wonderful transgender woman as a daughter-in-law, so I apologize in advance if my portrayal of Eddie is offensive by today's standards; I believe Marion's kindness to the character reflects her own acceptance of diversity.

Shortly after I sent off the gift story, I received this note from her:

Delight is right; I read this with shrieks of joy, and Lisa demanded to know what I was screaming about. This—er—thing was the answer. Thanks for giving me such a good laugh. – Marion.

Those who knew Marion personally may recognize one of her favorite sayings in the final scene. Also the Cabbage Patch dolls.

A Heat Wave in
the Hellers

D espite the gentle chill of spring, a fire burned in the
ancient tower high in Comyn Castle. Regis Hastur stared
into its flickering depths, the orange light tinting his flowing
white hair, and found no comfort there. He sat in the same chair
his grandfather, Danvan Hastur of Hastur, had used when he
too had wrestled with Darkover's fate. Every splinter of wood,
every thread of tapestry, every bit of *laran*-mined metal reeked
of centuries of Hastur tradition, Hastur responsibility. Regis
hated the room even as he drew strength from it, and for this
reason he had insisted on it, rather than one of the less formal
chambers, for today's meeting.

A light tap, courteous but not timid, and the door swung
open to admit Danilo Syrtis, dark-eyed and unsmiling, wearing
the colors of the Ardais Domain, of which he was Regent. Regis
leapt to his feet.

"She's here, Dani? You've seen her? Is she comfortable in
her quarters? The *coridom* wasn't sure what a woman of the
Terranan would need."

"Yes, and yes, and yes. Please calm down, Regis. Dan

Lawton cleared up the mess at Terran Customs, and they'll all be here in a few minutes."

Regis stalked back to his chair and sat down, his fingers unconsciously tracing the intricate carvings of the arm rests. Even in stillness, his still-youthful features retained an edge of tension. He drew a deep breath. "What do you think? Can she help us? Was I a fool to send for her?"

Danilo moved about the room, checking the chairs of age-darkened wood that had been arranged into a rough circle long before he'd been born. "All Darkover is in your debt, *vai dom*. Nobody would dare call you a fool."

"Oh yes, the great Regis Hastur can do no wrong!"

Danilo paused and said gently, "Are you afraid you've made a mistake this time, *bredu*? No one expects you to be infallible. Besides, you had to try something new. Neither our *laran* powers nor the *Terranan* technology have had any effect so far, and even Andrea Closson didn't know about all the surprises her enterprising minions created."

There came another knock at the door, and Danilo ushered in Linnea Storn-Lanart and Doctor Jason Allison. Linnea, stern and lovely in the robes of a Tower-trained *leronis*, nodded to Danilo and greeted Regis with formal courtesy. She brushed her fingertips across the back of his wrist, a telepath's fleeting touch that told Regis that behind her icy reserve, she was as deeply disturbed as he.

"Please sit down, Jason," said Regis. "We're all friends here, and this is our toughest challenge yet. I'm counting on you, all of you."

"What's this surprise Dani hinted at?" Jason Allison asked.

Just then, Dan Lawton, the Terran Legate, arrived, escorting a short, comfortably round middle-aged woman. Unlike most

Terranan, she seemed quite relaxed in the full skirts and loose tunic of traditional Darkovan women's clothing. Her hair, cropped short like a Renunciate's, looked almost reddish in contrast to her dark blue and gray tartans.

"You lend us grace, *Domna* Miriam," said Regis. "Pardon me if I mispronounce your name—the transliteration is a little difficult."

"*Z'par servu*," the *Terranan* woman replied in perfectly inflected *casta*. She sat down and rearranged the layers of her shawl. "Well, Regis, you've gotten yourself into a fine pickle here."

"Then you are already acquainted with the particulars of our crisis?"

"Not at all," replied Marion Zimmer Bradley. "I know you wouldn't have hauled me all the way here—across half the galaxy and heaven knows how many centuries—without a good reason. It can't be either psychic or ecological, or your Telepath Council, with the resources of the now-defunct World Wrecker Corporation, could have handled it without all this fanfare. What's the problem?"

"We're not sure if it's one or several," Regis said, "but they all have to do with changes in Darkover's climate. The Terran Meteorological Service people have been helping us to survey the changes."

"The first sign we got of any trouble was coastal flooding," Dan Lawton said. "Temora and Dalereuth often experience high tides when the orbits of the four moons bring them into alignment, but this time there was no conjunction. The other changes were so subtle at first, they were attributed to seasonal variability. Our meteorological people were stunned at the melting rate of the great Hellers glacier."

"And the blizzards in the Dry Towns," Linnea added. Her heart-shaped face was set and grim, but her voice was perfectly calm. "It was all we could do to convince them this was not a curse we Comyn 'witches' had laid on them."

"As you may know, the Comyn have limited regional weather control," Regis said, "but we use it only with the greatest care and in cases of critical need. If we bring storm clouds to put out a forest fire in one place, it may cause a drought in another. But to do such a thing on a planetary scale—no Tower circle alive today is capable of it."

"It sounds to me like Darkover has shifted its planetary axis," said Marion. "No, nobody leaked the answer, but it's obvious. I'm not entirely unfamiliar with the principles of planetary physics. The question is, what could cause such a thing?"

"And how can it be reversed?" added Danilo.

"Not by anything the Terran Empire possesses, or ever possessed," the Legate commented. "The geophysical experts suggested using shaped nuclear charges to tilt the planet back. But it's never been tried on such a scale before, only on a few asteroids in the Vega system, and it might backfire in the other direction. If it didn't blast Darkover into an entirely new orbit."

"Or rain radioactive debris over half the planet," Jason Allison added.

"Which leaves us where we Comyn have always been, left to our own resources," Regis said. "Dani, you've been searching the records at Hali. Did you find anything useful there?"

"Not within formal Domains history, I'm afraid. If the Comyn ever developed *laran* talents on that vast a scale, they were lost a long time ago. But there were fragments of still older records, dating back as far as the Ages of Chaos. I found some legends of a young girl who apparently had the ability to tap into the planet's magnetic field, but she was confined to a matrix-bound stasis field after a series of calamities."

"How much detail is given?" Linnea asked. "If there's a factual basis to the story, if we could track down her location, we might find some way, with our current *laran* technology, to de-activate the matrix field and—"

"Absolutely not!" Marion sprang to her feet. "I will *not* allow you to resurrect Dorilys. In fact, I specifically forbid you to do so. I've had enough adolescent hysteria for one lifetime. Besides, it's a terrible idea. What little self-control she had was burnt out ages ago. No one but a raving idiot would consider letting her loose. You'd do better asking Sharra herself for help."

She turned and shook her finger at Regis. "Nor will I bring Jaelle back, marry off Dyan Ardais, import Mister Spock, dig a tunnel under New York, or anything else of that ilk!"

No one said anything for a long moment, since it was well known that Lord Ardais had perished in the last fatal clash between the Sharra matrix and the legendary Sword of Aldones, which was why Danilo Syrtis was currently Regent of Ardais. Who or what the other things were, Regis had no idea.

Linnea blinked politely, too much a comynara to say anything more than, "Your pardon, *Domna* Miriam. I meant no offense."

Marion sat down again and replied in a calmer voice, "No, my dear, it's I who must apologize. I suppose I should take it as a compliment, and I dearly love to encourage young writers. But some days I sympathize with Conan Doyle when he tried to kill Sherlock Holmes by throwing him off Reichenbach Falls."

"Yes, he would be very upset if something so terrible befell his friend," Linnea commented in a puzzled voice.

"What about the Sharra matrix?" Marion asked. "That was

certainly powerful enough to distort a planetary axis. What about the places that had been attuned to it—has there been any activity there? That would tell us if anyone's been tinkering with those forces."

"None of the Towers has reported anything like that," said Linnea, whose work in the relays gave her access to such information.

Marion thought a moment. "I don't suppose Lew Alton is available to check on it for us?"

"I'm sorry, *Domna* Miriam, he's still off-planet," Danilo replied.

"I can't blame him, after all he's been through, although I would have liked to see Marja while she was still little enough to cuddle. I suppose I'm the best one to do it, then. If you could supply me with a guide, I'll inspect the local sites myself."

There were no more suggestions, other than to continue the research efforts at Hali and with Terran Geophysical. The meeting adjourned. Marion lingered behind for a private word with Regis. He turned to her and said, "I'm not sure I should let you go alone, *Domna* Miriam. It's too much to ask of a guest."

"You didn't cart me all the way here just for a panel discussion, did you?" Marion demanded. "Or do you mean it's too much to ask of a woman?"

"Not that," Regis answered. "Just the old fear that if we let someone else solve our present problems, we become incapable of dealing with our future problems."

Marion nodded, her eyes somber. "I know how deeply worried you are. The World Wrecker disasters are too recent, too raw in everyone's memories. But you must believe me, Regis, this world is as precious to me as it is to you. What began as the daydream of a lonely child has grown to a rich and varied planet, home to many different visions. Something tells me that this time I will be only a piece of the solution."

Regis studied the woman, the steadiness in her eyes, heard how she spoke from her heart. "I would not have been so fearful for Darkover's fate if I had known we had such friends," he said.

The tap sounded hesitant, even through the thick wooden door. Marion looked up from her half-read book with a mixture of annoyance and relief. She'd barely started unpacking, having refused to let the *kyrri* organize her carefully chaotic arrangements, and here she was having to repack again. After many trips to the Terran Hebrides, she knew she couldn't go exploring on Darkover without her down-lined boots, and they were buried somewhere, probably underneath the sweaters. But it was not the boots that harried her, making it impossible for her to settle down and work, it was the bone-deep fear she'd sensed in all of them this morning. Even Linnea, with her *leronis* calm, enough to make a Vulcan seem sentimental. Even Regis.

She put down the book she'd been reading to distract herself and reached for the door latch.

No sooner had she touched it than the door flew open and a slender figure threw itself at her feet, arms tightly locked around her knees. Marion's knees were not up to this treatment at the best of times, and certainly not after so many hours on an interstellar flight. She gazed at the short-cropped hair, the trail-worn tunic and distinctive low boots, and deduced that some Free Amazon was using this undignified method of appealing to her for help. She loosened the hands from her legs and said gently,

"You need not kneel to me, child. No harm shall come to any woman while I am able to prevent it."

The Renunciate looked up, pale and tear-stained. The eyes were huge and gray, the thin face smudged. "On your Oath as a Guild Mother, I claim your protection."

"I've already said you were safe here. Now get off the floor so we can talk sensibly."

Marion cleared away the nearest chair, moving aside three more half-read books. She sat her visitor in it and held out a mug of warmed wine. "Get that in your tummy and tell me what the problem is."

"You know what we suffer here, you of all women!" The voice was tight with emotion, but low-pitched and resonant enough to make Marion wonder about formal voice training. "Take me away with you, far from this place of oppression!"

"I had no idea things were so bad for the Guild. Is this some recent change of affairs, perhaps tied in with the climate changes? People are always looking for a scapegoat when times are bad."

"No, you don't understand! If I stay here I'll die! The only one I've ever loved has gone into space and I'll never—never see—" The words broke off into heart-rending sobs. Marion offered the packet of tissues from her suitcase and sat down in the other chair, prepared to listen to a long story.

"You have no idea what I've been through—"

"I have some understanding of the love-stricken heart," Marion said sympathetically, "not all of it academic."

"I never knew what it was to be alive until my love opened my eyes. I'd even saved enough for the fare, but those monsters—they won't let me leave! They're so threatened by a woman's discovery of her true nature that they've kept me penned here, dying of a broken heart! By all the gods, you've got to help me get off this disgusting ball of dust where women are treated worse than dirt!"

Marion thought this was being a little melodramatic, but she'd observed the same phenomena in Terran teenagers. Generally, when left to their own devices they grew out of it. She said, as reasonably as possible, "Surely Darkover has enough troubles without adding to yours. Perhaps I can talk to the Terran authorities for you. What is your name, and where do you need passage to?"

"Eduartia, that's how I'm called. I've got to get to Gor, to where a woman's secret needs are truly understood—"

"To *where?*" Marion turned peach-colored.

The door flew open once again. Two women and a man, dressed in the robes of Tower healers, rushed in. Eduartia scrambled up, screamed "You'll never take me alive!" and dove between them for the door.

The man and the taller of the women wrestled Eduartia to the ground while the second woman drew out her starstone and held it over Eduartia's forehead.

"We mean you no harm," she said in a soft, almost hypnotic voice. "We're here to help—relax, don't fight us—we're your friends..."

Eduartia arched and bucked, but was held fast. Finally the power of the healer's matrix overcame all resistance.

"May I inquire what you think you're doing?" Marion asked when it was quiet enough to get a word in. "She appealed to me for help—"

"She?" The smaller *leronis* stood up, her hair loosened from its butterfly clasp and curling around her head like a coppery aura. "I'm afraid you have been deceived, *mestra*. That's no woman, that's crazy Eddie dressed up like one. He usually picks something fairly harmless for his acting-out. This year he's got delusions of romanticism, ever since the Trade Delegation permitted importation of pseudo-pornography."

"Surely reading such trash wasn't sufficient to unbalance him," said Marion. "I may not find any redeeming value in the stuff, but I'll be the first to defend Don Wollheim's right to publish it."

"No," the taller *leronis* said, "but he's descended from Kyril Ardais through a *nedestro* line that wed into a fundamentalist *cristoforo* family. They're all unstable, but not dangerous. He wouldn't have attacked you—"

"Just tried to convince me to get him passage to Gor!"

"Is there such a place?"

"Heaven knows, I hope not. But even though it was under false pretenses, he did appeal to me for help, and I did agree. I'm afraid you'll have to leave him here with me until he himself is ready to leave."

"*Mestra*, you can't be serious."

Marion put her hands on her hips and stuck out her chin. "Try me."

"We'll have him back in custody, even if our Keeper has to appeal to Regis Hastur himself."

"Good!" said Marion, and closed the door firmly after them.

A short time later, a somewhat muddle-headed Eduart sat up and stared as Marion began stuffing her warmest clothing into the saddlebags. "You can either come with me or you can go back to the Tower," she said. "Personally, I don't care."

"You didn't let them take me..."

"Which you certainly deserved, after lying to me like that! I think my charity reflects more on me than on you."

156

Eduart pulled himself into the nearest empty chair. "I don't know why I do things like this. Act like I've got my own private Ghost Wind. I never mean to. Sometimes I think I should just let the healers fix my mind. They say I'd be just like everyone else."

Marion set aside the partly packed saddlebags and listened intently. "Why should the Tower healers want to make you like everyone else? The *leronis* said you don't hurt anyone."

"They used to just help through the rough times, and in between I find work in the Terran Zone. Then—everyone was talking about how things were so bad, we'd just have to get the *Terranan* in—and things changed."

"Darkover resisted becoming just another planet in the Terran Empire," Marion said thoughtfully, "but didn't escape an even more insidious threat. If there's anything the Terrans excel at, it's their ability to turn individuals into pablum-minded robots. Think the same, act the same, feel the same. Buy the same. I wonder why the healers fell for it."

Eduart looked down, blushing. "It could have been because of—well, it was meant as a joke!"

Marion didn't need to ask what "it" was, she'd heard the joke about the Dry Towner, the *leronis* and the *Terranan*, in several different versions. The joke must have hit too close to home, and even the Towers sometimes had egos to bruise. She sat back in her chair, rubbing her chin absently and thinking. At first she'd thought of Eduart as a minor distraction, but the parallel between his plight and Darkover's kept niggling at her, like a plotline she hadn't quite figured out yet. Were the changes in Darkover's climate—heat waves where there should be blizzards—a metaphor for enforced conformity? What a ridiculous idea!

❖ · ❖ · ❖

Marion had planned her route to cover all the accessible locations in a single circuit. The final Sharra locus was a pretty spot, a sheltered valley dotted with trees, about a half-day's travel from Thendara. Eduart set out their trail lunch while Marion scouted around, located the place once attuned to the deadly fire matrix, and determined that it had been inactive for a number of years.

She propped herself against a rock, enjoying the sensation of not being mounted on a horse. Regis had done his best for her with a gentle old mare of excellent Alton breeding, whose sweet temper and soft gaits would be suitable for even a pregnant woman, but Marion had too much personal acquaintance with cleaning up after horses to feel very romantic about being upon one. She wished there were a hot tub here, but the gentle sunshine made an acceptable substitute.

Eduart wiped the last of the nut-bread crumbs from his hands and offered Marion some more *jaco*. "If only we could have weather like Valeron." He groaned. "They have cool breezes now, not this everlasting heat."

Marion didn't bother opening her eyes. "Two days ago we had cold winds, and all you could talk about was getting warm again. Can't you make up your mind?"

"What would be the point of being satisfied with what you already have?" he said.

Marion sighed, mounted up, and turned her horse's head back towards Thendara.

After a long soak in a steaming bath, she felt considerably less depressed. The Sharra loci had been uniformly inactive, which scotched her first theory, but now she had formulated a new idea of how Darkover's planetary axis might have been shifted.

"I don't see how we can convince them," Marion murmured as she tucked her Cabbage Patch dolls in for the night. "But I'm sure you'll think of something by morning."

After breakfast, Regis was anxious to hear what Marion found. She dismissed the negative results of her expedition and began giving orders for a banquet, "to be arranged as soon as possible. The future of all Darkover depends upon this meal!" Guest lists, accommodations, "a full-sized circus tent–it's very important that as many guests as possible be within view of each other," and a detailed menu were all forthcoming at such a rapid rate that Danilo had to fetch two additional scribes to get it all down accurately.

"I've never heard of such a concoction," Regis said after she'd repeated her instructions for the main dish three times. "Are you sure it's edible?"

"I can guarantee that your own ancestors put away more of it than I care to imagine," she replied, smiling. "Can we get it all done quickly? It may take some time for the effect to reverse itself, and the sooner we start, the better."

"We can use Terran air transport to deliver the invitations and convey the guests," Danilo said. "Lawton did promise his full cooperation. As for the feast itself…"

"If you and Regis can't pull it off, then no one on Darkover can," Marion assured him.

Marion glanced up with satisfaction at the patchwork of brilliant synthetic panels that the Terran Parachute Squad suppliers had rigged into an immense pavilion. From her vantage point on the central dais, she looked down on the equally colorful crowd that was even now settling down to the banquet. Town leaders and *Comhi-Letzii* Guild Mothers from the principal Houses rubbed shoulders with mountain lairds in skins and tartans and Dry Town magnates in their garish finery. The remnants of the old Comyn Council were interspersed with *Terranan*, including Dan Lawton and his highest-ranking aides.

Regis leaned over to speak to Marion and saw her eyes brimming with either laughter or mischief, he couldn't tell which. "This had better work. Darkover hasn't seen this much power in one place at one time since–"

"Don't worry, just eat your dinner and tell me what you think of it."

Regis cut a sliver of the glistening sausage and took a hesitant bite. "I've eaten worse on the fire lines, or–Dani?"

Danilo grabbed for his wine goblet and swallowed convulsively, tears streaming from his eyes. He grasped the insulated starstone at his throat and closed his eyes, clearly concentrating. When he opened them again, he was able to speak, although his complexion remained pea-colored. "That was–the foulest–*mess*–I've ever–had the misfortune–to taste."

"It's not that bad," Regis said.

Danilo muttered through his clenched teeth. Marion could not understand his words, but Regis clearly caught the telepathic drift of it.

"Don't be hard on Dani," said Linnea as she laid down her three-tined fork. "I rather agree with him."

Marion, who had been intently watching the guests at the

160

adjacent tables, chuckled. A round-bellied magnate of the Pan-Darkovan League had just transferred his entire portion to the plate of his neighbor, a yellow-mustached Dry Towner, who struggled to convey his gratitude in barely understandable *cahuenga*. Marion heard the words, "delightful morsel." Throughout the vast pavilion, similar exchanges were taking place as the guests reacted to the food with everything from thinly veiled disgust to outright gluttony.

"You see?" said Jason Allison, farther down the table. "It's not gourmet fare, but it's highly nutritious." To emphasize his point, he took a large mouthful.

"If you feel that way about it, you can eat mine." Linnea shoved her plate in his direction.

The Terran doctor regarded the double portion and shook his head. "I'm not *that* hungry."

"Oh dear. *Domna* Miriam, is it truly necessary that we—that we—" The normally self-contained comynara struggled to retain her composure in the face of the main dish.

Understanding broke out on Regis's face like sunshine following a storm. "Of course not! That's the point of this exercise, isn't it? To show us how different we each are—"

He broke off as a young cadet darted to his side and whispered a message. As his face relaxed into a broad smile, it seemed that the weight of years lifted from him. He stood, and the crowd grew silent, expectant.

"News from Neskaya Tower, my friends. It is snowing in the Hellers."

Late that evening, once the guests had either returned home

or to suitable quarters, Regis stretched out in his most comfort-able armchair before a merry fire. Marion sat opposite him, her feet propped on a cushioned hassock.

"When I discovered the Sharra places were inactive, I realized that the planetary shifts had to be human in origin," she explained. "Your people couldn't locate anyone responsible, so it wasn't the work of a small group of powerful telepaths. Which left, logically, a very large group with only minimal *laran*."

"Practically anyone on the planet."

"It was Eddie who showed me how it might work–always wanting things to be other than they were–hot when it was cold, cool when it was warm, dry when it rained. Wherever we were, he wanted to be someplace else."

"I suppose the World Wreckers crisis opened the way for that," Regis observed. "People all over Darkover wanted someone to wave a magic wand and solve their problems for them. The banquet taught us an appreciation of our own diversity, instead of envying what everyone else had. Since we all ate the same revolting dish, the unhappiness had to come from us, ourselves, not the food itself."

Marion nodded. "Yes, people learn rather quickly on a visceral level. And fortunately for Darkover, the haggis shortage was not yet upon us."

About the Author

Deborah J. Ross is an award-nominated writer and editor of fantasy and science fiction, with over a dozen traditionally published novels and five dozen short stories in print. Recent releases include *Thunderlord* and *The Children of Kings* (with Marion Zimmer Bradley); *Collaborators* (Lambda Literary Finalist, as Deborah Wheeler), and *The Seven-Petaled Shield* trilogy. Her short fiction has appeared in *F & SF, Asimov's, Star Wars: Tales from Jabba's Palace*, and the Book View Café anthology, *Nevertheless She Persisted*, and has earned honorable mention in *Year's Best SF*. She has served as Secretary to the Science Fiction Fantasy Writers of America (SFWA), is a member of Book View Café, and chaired the jury for the Philip K. Dick Award. When she's not writing, she knits for charity, plays classical piano, and studies yoga.

Also by Deborah J. Ross

Darkover novels (with Marion Zimmer Bradley)
The Laran Gambit (forthcoming)
Thunderlord
The Children of Kings
Hastur Lord
The Alton Gift
A Flame in Hali
Zandru's Forge
The Fall of Neskaya

The Seven-Petaled Shield trilogy
The Heir of Khored
Shannivar
The Seven-Petaled Shield

*Collaborators** (forthcoming)
*Northlight**
*Jaydium**

Collections
*Transfusion and Other Tales of Hope**
*Azkhantian Tales**
*Other Doorways: Early Novels**
*Pearls of Fire, Dreams of Steel**

Nonfiction
*Ink Dance, Essays on the Writing Life**

*available in BVC editions

ABOUT BOOK VIEW CAFÉ

Book View Café Publishing Cooperative is an author-owned cooperative of over fifty professional writers, publishing in a variety of genres such as fantasy, romance, mystery, and science fiction.

BVC authors include *New York Times* and *USA Today* bestsellers; Nebula, Hugo, and Philip K. Dick Award winners; World Fantasy Award, Campbell Award, and RITA Award nominees; and winners and nominees of many other publishing awards.

Since its debut in 2008, BVC has gained a reputation for producing high-quality e-books, and is now bringing that same quality to its print editions.